Tombstone

A Western Novel

Richard G. Hole

Far West 4

At that time the Indians of the famous Geronimo still roamed that part of the basin and staying in towns close to their hidden shelters was extremely dangerous due to the "raids" that the fearsome Redskins used to carry out from time to time.

Some desperate for life, a handful of brave people without fear of anything or anyone, and several nomads from the region, had instinctively gathered there, forming a near-town that managed to survive perhaps by a miracle or because the Indians, without giving them importance , they respected them.

But the unexpected discovery of the Tombstone mines changed the landscape there in a matter of months.

Tombstone is a story belonging to the Far West collection, a collection of novels developed in the American Wild West.

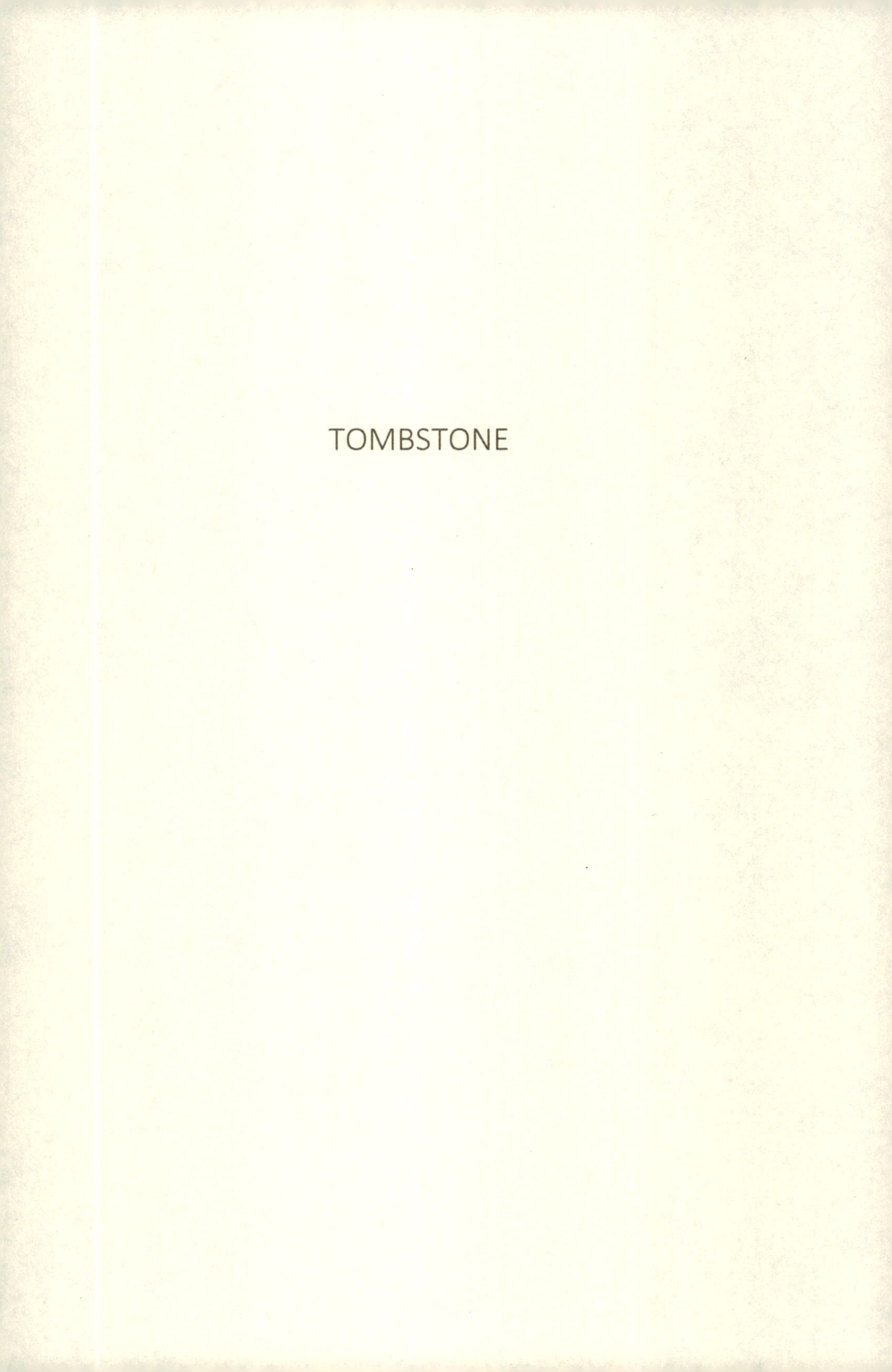

TOMBSTONE

Fairbank had been until a very short time ago a miserable town in the southeast of Arpona, with hardly any relief and with a very scarce neighborhood. At that time the Indians of the famous Geronimo still roamed that part of the basin and staying in towns close to their hidden shelters was extremely dangerous due to the "raids" that the fearsome Redskins used to carry out from time to time.

Some desperate for life, a handful of brave people without fear of anything or anyone, and several nomads from the region, had instinctively gathered there, forming a near-town that managed to survive perhaps by a miracle or because the Indians, without giving them importance , they respected them.

But the unexpected discovery of the Tombstone mines changed the landscape there in a matter of months. The influx of adventurers materially turning to the mining fields, populated that, although in an unstable way, subject to what the mines were capable of sustaining and, although the town that took the name of the mines was erected in weeks, acquiring too dense a population volume, under its protection and, due to the proximity of the deposits, Fairbank took on a sudden importance and what just before were a few ramshackle and unstable huts, began to become a series of buildings much more capable, more solid in presentation and in a number that was beginning to scare its primitive neighbors.

Like salmon, on their return to the fresh waters of the rivers they need a haven to acclimatize to fresh water, so many adventurers who flocked to the famous mines, stuck in Fairbank to orient themselves and some even preferred the populated because their activities were far from wells and excavations.

Mining towns generally consisted of fifty percent rough and tough men who indulged in the backbreaking work of mining the land to support another fifty percent more clever beings than, with their ingenuity, skill, or, appealing in harsher and less scrupulous means, they knew how to live off the labor of the slaves of the land.

And part of this contingent had taken possession of Fairbank, because to report to Tombstone, if they needed it, it was enough to take a walk of a few miles.

For the traffickers of all kinds of goods to be supplied to the miners, Fairbank was safer and more comfortable than Tombstone itself. There they could install their warehouses and warehouses with more security, receive the merchandise that descended from Tucson in wagons and prepare them for the mining town and there some had their houses, without this depriving them of being in contact with the harsh town.

One of the first who managed to see clearly the beautiful future that Fairbank would offer him without having to suffer the onslaught of the mining hordes below, was Grant Phelps, who hastened to build a large bar with all its accessories to facilitate lounging and entertainment for the new inhabitants of the town, without them being able to miss in their establishment anything that others similar could offer them in Tombstone.

There, good and bad whiskey was dispatched, according to the economic state of the client; there was jin, gin, rum and other drinks; There were gambling tables there for those with a fortune to lose and for those with only a dollar to distract with playing cards, and even a few girls might be found there willing to serve rough customers with pleasure and make them more pleasant. hours of fun.

Many things were told about Phelps without absolute certainty. It was said that not long before he was a penniless adventurer who had become rich overnight, thus managing to install that luxurious gambling den and quite violent feats were told of him, since apparently his career in the West had been bumpy and quite agitated.

The absolute truth of her life was unknown, but a part of it had to be admitted. A man who dared to open an establishment of that kind in such a rough place, had to be very imposed in that environment and also be a man to whom the eye of a colt presented head-on at any moment would not make him tremble a little or a lot of.

Grant was a man in his late fifties. Despite his age and short stature, since his height was quite medium, he was strong as a bull. He was relatively thick, but fat-free, dark to the point of looking Mexican, and he had nothing to thank Mother Nature for, for his face was crude, pockmarked, with a piggy nose, bulging eyes, and puffy, rude lips.

Grant was known to be unappealing, but he tried to soften his ugliness by shaving daily, combing his thick black hair with shiny cosmetics, and dressing as elegantly as his figure allowed.

His establishment made no distinction between customers. The ostentatious and the raggedy had a place in it if they had enough money to cover the expense, but among this strange clientele those most prominent elements of whom it was known or suspected that their activities were extensive and of the most outstanding stood out and were treated amicably. dirtier, despite the fact that there were few things morally clean there.

This friendly preference for certain types spread the rumor that Grant was involved, albeit in the shadows, in all kinds of business outside his establishment, but this, like his record, only he and some of the others knew with certainty. his friends.

* * *

Tyson Winslow, was a product of Eastern North America whom the hangover of life had thrown over the vicinity of the deposits, as the storm throws the plank of a fragile boat destroyed by the storm.

He had been born and raised in Boston, there he began his studies when he was the son of a haberdashery merchant and there he was plunged into misery, when his father, going bankrupt in the business, decided not to survive the mine and voluntarily suppressed of the census.

Tyson, somewhat disoriented and inexperienced in life, lost his composure and to defend himself accepted a position as a traveling jewelry traveler in the western regions.

He had no ability to convince anyone and his order notes were so poor that one day he received a terse letter from the house he represented. In view of his uselessness, he was separated from his position and had to use it as best he could to continue living, but not at the expense of the factory.

And the boy, twenty-two years old and with a poor life experience, found himself abandoned in the middle of Arizona, with hardly a few coins in his pocket and with a very wrong concept of what it was to settle there and work on things that I did not understand.

He rolled like a ball from town to town applying for jobs he wasn't worth. He had to work as a laborer in fields or haciendas, he wasted bending his waist on farms and crops, he went hungry and deprived, and never managed to dispose of a single dollar that was not absolutely essential for his poor maintenance.

Until one day he learned that Tombstone was the paradise of illusions who dream of making a fortune in a few hours. There the earth dumped tons of silver on the adventurers who only had to appear there to collect it and, without taking further information regarding the case, he decided to appear in the mining field ready to be one of the favorites of fortune.

But when, after a thousand toils, he managed to reach the country of Jauja, he suffered the disappointment of knowing something about what it means to be a miner. This required practice, a team to endure and work, provisions to sustain itself while a seam to be exploited was found, and many other things that it lacked and that surely it would never be able to provide itself.

And after a very brief and eventful visit to the bronco town, he decided to abandon it. He had heard of Fairbank, where silver was not mined, but there was a need for people to work, and he had moved there in the hope of finding a job of whatever kind. He lacked money and life there reached a level of fright.

"Tombstone Bar," as Grant had called his joint, caught his eye. There were waiters at the counter and in the kitchen serving meals for the adjoining canteen; it would take people to wash dishes and perform some other vulgar chores, and since the need was pressing, his interest was to talk to Phelps and beg him to provide him with any job, however rude, so that he could survive without being given over to despair or pillage.

Tyson had made a few visits to the joint during the day in order to approach its owner. The nightlife of the place frightened him and he also understood that these were not hours to distract the smart and emphatic owner. He had much more to attend to than to take care of a poor castaway of life as he was.

But the sunlight rhymed little with Grant's habits and business demands, and his visits had been fruitless. To talk to him, she needed to look for him from midnight onwards and Tyson, that night in early spring, was wandering through the dense and rough town killing time while waiting for the long-awaited hour to speak with Grant.

He felt terribly hungry, for he had not carried anything to his stomach for almost two days and he told himself desperately that, if the owner of the joint did not want to attend to him and offer him something to earn a living, starvation would make him faint on the dust of the road. .

In that exasperating wait, Tyson had walked the misaligned and winding streets of the town several times and it was approximately eleven o'clock when, attracted by a certain establishment, he stopped in front of him.

It was a figon where meals were served in abundance. The place, not very spacious, looked very crowded. The tables were huddled with customers, devouring the conduit eagerly as if they were as hungry as he was, and Tyson had stared at them with deep envy during their passes in front of the door.

He was drawn to and comforted by the smell of melted tallow emanating from the hidden kitchen. A rather foul odor that was partly neutralized by the softer and more appetizing bacon.

The figon, for a better appeal, had a window with a solid wire mesh in the absence of glass and behind that metallic prison and on the board, cans of preserves were piled up, some sausages, some sliced hams that had acquired quite a purple color. suspicious and some pieces of bison that, losing their bleeding color, turned pale pink and as bait to a legion of well-nourished flies that swarmed over them.

Tyson, facing the window, gazed wide-eyed at those appealing delicacies and his stomach felt more aggressive and his tongue clicked dry at the impossible feast before him.

To console himself, he had provided himself with a thin branch that he pounded between his hard teeth. He could taste the bitter taste of the harsh substitute, but it seemed to give hunger comforting.

And unconsciously, he separated the branch from his mouth and inserted it through the gaps in the mesh until he reached one of the pieces of meat with the tip. She couldn't dream of luring it in and pulling it out into pieces through the small gaps, but she set about pricking the piece and after plunging the tip of the stick into it, pulling it out and taking it to her mouth to suck. It tasted like meat and this seemed to comfort him a little more.

And he gave himself up with such eagerness to that task that he lost the notion of reality, abstracting himself in such a way that he did not realize what was around him.

He was devoted to this strange task, when behind him and full of curiosity a very remarkable guy stopped that Tyson had not yet discovered in the town.

He was a tall and thin man, who must have already reached the age of fifty-eight.

In his youth he must have been an elegant and graceful man and also handsome, because despite the fact that the years had mistreated him a lot, he retained features that were accused of what he was in his good times.

Her face was pale and smooth, her eyes gray and melancholic, her nose perfect, and her lips thin and bloodless.

He had thick hair of long, silky gray hair that spilled out at the back to touch the collar of his frock coat, and a fine, well-groomed mustache made the expression on his face even more graceful.

He wore a wide gray frock coat with airy skirts, a white vest with colorful spots, and tube trousers that hid part of his well-polished boots. The shirt was white and closed with a soft collar and under it, a scarf in the shape of a butterfly.

His head was untouched, which gave him a more attractive air, and his hands were long, thin, with very agile and very white fingers.

They all knew him at Fairbank; his name was Cosimo La-more "if that was his real name" and he acted as a gambler at the most important table in Phelps's joint.

Cosimo stared at Tyson and instantly guessed the boy's tragedy. A tragedy that affected many, but that most solved less prosaically, not settling for sucking the tip of a branch inserted into a piece of meat.

And approaching him he asked softly:

"Excellent banquet, isn't it? You may need a bottle of baking soda to digest.

Tyson, embarrassed as a misguided schoolboy, turned and with broken words, muttered:

"Excuse me, I didn't realize it and ...

He wanted to escape, but Cosimo, grabbing him by the arm, stopped him. His pressure, although slight, gave the young man the feeling that it had been done with a pliers.

"Don't run away, boy. I am not the owner of those rubbish and I cannot complain about it.

Then, lovingly, without letting go, she asked:

"Very hungry, boy?

He was ashamed to confess it. A vigorous young man humbled himself by acknowledging that he was dying of necessity with no means to earn it.

"Oh no! He "stammered." It was a mechanical thing. I already ate ...

"How many days has it been since your last meal?

He did not feel the courage to continue lying and confessed:

"Two.

"Wow. For a young stomach like yours it is too much torment. I suppose that a couple of pieces of that meat that, although a bit old, would still be eaten, a piece of bacon, some cake and a glass of beer would leave you feeling like new, right?

Tyson pleaded:

"Don't tease me by tormenting me more. I am not lazy and I am looking for work, but until now I have not found it. I came wrong believing that being a miner was something simpler and easier, and now I am stuck here with no means to go anywhere. I am looking for something where I can win the most precise and I am able to accept the lowest in order to solve the problem.

"The lowest thing, boy, is to go out on the trail to assault a miner or rob one in the darkness of a street.

"I was not referring to that, but to work.

"Well, you might find it, but it will get you so exhausted that you won't be able to lift a feather from the ground. Pass in there with me.

"I can not; I told him I don't have a job and I don't have a penny either and ...

"I invite you, boy. I am not an altruist to feed all the hungry here in Fairbank and I would not either, even if I could, because most of them do not deserve the junk I leave at lunchtime, but you seem different to me. I will help you for tonight to solve your problem and who knows if tomorrow you will be worth it alone to solve it.

"Oh, I don't know how to thank you! I don't know anyone here to lend me a dollar, but when I work I will pay them back.

"You won't bother with that, boy. I do not do charity with revenue and I can afford to pay you a dinner and several. I earn a lot and I don't have to worry about what I put behind my back, because my back is free of weight. Come on, come on.

And he pulled him into the figon.

A table had just been vacated and Cosimo led the boy to it. Soon Tyson realized that his patron was an important figure in the town, because the sticky waiter who came to attend him welcomed him warmly and with respect.

"Good evening, Mr. Lamore" he greeted. As usual?

"If the same. In addition, you will serve this somewhat listless boy two good chunks of roast beef with potatoes, some fried bacon, but quite tall, a good slice of cake, and a baked apple. Also put him a mug of beer in case he has trouble swallowing all that.

The waiter smiled sympathetically. Apparently this was not an isolated case in the generous life of the gambler.

"Understood, Mr. Lamore. I will order that the meat is quite abundant.

"Yes, and start serving him something promptly, because if he doesn't say that his little appetite will go away.

He spoke jokingly, but with joy, without the intention of annoying or hurting the boy's feelings, and the boy, with glazed eyes that leaned out and struggled to burst out with tears of infinite gratitude, did not know how to thank Lamore for his providential help.

While Cosimo ate very little and almost reluctantly, Tyson eagerly devoured the strong stuff that had been served to him. It had been a long time since she had had a glut of that nature, and her gratitude to the gambler rose sharply as her stomach filled to the brim.

Cosimo glanced at him, but didn't ask him any questions. He let him calm his hunger, but he smiled with satisfaction. For him, that moment would not have changed for the most successful one with some cards in hand.

When the apple dessert was served, Cosimo asked:

"From the East, friend?

"Yes sir; from Boston.

"I figured it out from the way he spoke. Nice population.

"Do you know her?

"I know many cities; sometimes I think that there are many more than what it would have been convenient for me to know, but you don't have to worry about me. What was it like to fall into this hell, boy?

Tyson gave him an account of his life and when he finished the story, the gambler commented:

"I realize, but I think this is not the most conducive environment for you. Hopefully, you will not go from washing dishes in a kitchen, unless you decide to follow the example of others.

"Not my idea, sir. I would like to work, save something and leave this. I would more like to work on a farm, although I already acted in one and they told me it was useless.

"Everything is a question of patience and will. Here, well, I don't know ... what is your idea?

"The same one that you pointed out. Ask for a modest dishwasher job or something similar.

"There are not many places to choose ... What is your name?

"Tyson Winslow. I know there are few, but I had thought to ask the owner of the Tombstone Bar for a job. The place is big, it has a lot of work and maybe ...

"Hmm! I do not know. I know Grant well and I will tell you that as a master he is rough as sand.

"But there is little to choose from. Do you say you know him?

"I work at his joint.

"What do you work with him? I believed...

He fell silent. Cosimo, smiling, indicated:

"What did you think?

"Oh nothing! I thought you would live independently. I can't imagine him working in that joint.

"Why not?

"Well, because ... his type, his air, his way of behaving are those of a gentleman and there these ...

"Gentlemen strike, okay, but I stopped being one a long time ago and I am in my environment; young guy. A gambler can never be better than in such a place.

"I take responsability. I'm sorry I said anything that ...

"You have not offended me. Each one accepts what fate imposes on him. Years ago, many years ago, I would have laughed if someone had predicted that I would come to the "Tombstone Bar" and yet you see ...

"Yes, yes," Tyson replied, flustered. Life imposes many sacrifices and you have to resign yourself. Who knows if one day we can get away from this.

"You, yes; you are young, vigorous, you must have yearnings, although luck has not let you think about the afterlife; But I ... my life declines, disappointments extinguished all illusions and only the materiality of living forces me to defend this stupid life so useless and dirty, but to which we cling as if it was really worth fighting for. I fell here, I stopped at this bump in the road and if I don't roll any more I know that I won't get up any higher either. You have to forget the past to live in the present and it is enough.

He consulted his watch hidden in the pocket of the branded vest protected by a thick gold chain and said:

"Sorry, boy, but I have to leave you. The time has come for me to act and that does not admit of delay.

"I understand you. I don't know how to thank you for what you have done for me tonight. It has lifted my spirits and now I feel able to fight fiercely to make my way. Maybe I'll see you when I go to talk to Mr. Phelps.

"You will see me, but you will not be able to speak to me, because during my work I still have few eyes to deal with him. Talk to Grant and when I finish tonight's job, if necessary, I'll talk to him too to recommend you. Now I won't be able to entertain myself.

"Thank you. I've already given you enough trouble.

"None, boy. If I can do something for you I will. See you around.

And with a graceful wave of the hand he said goodbye to Tyson.

The latter left the figon full and with a less gloomy air. At a crucial moment in her life, luck had shown itself propitious with the help of this strange but generous man, and this seemed a good omen. Perhaps Grant would also be humanitarian with him and offer him a job in his joint with which to start a new life.

After walking around the village, around twelve o'clock he made his way to the Tombstone Bar. The hour was propitious and the large venue was crowded with customers.

When he entered, the upright piano, reached there God knows by what efforts, was reeling a lilting melody and in the center, empty of tables, a few rude and rude miners danced like heavy bears with the girls, whose mission was none other than bear the roughness and weight of those mastodons.

A thunderous din hummed inside. Laughter, harsh voices, oaths, and loud calls were in contrast to the noise of glasses and bottles uncorking new drinks and the characteristic noise of dice. The music was relegated to the background as a background harmony.

Tyson entered fearfully. He had visited very few places of this kind and he felt in them like a strange fowl, apart from the fact that knowing that he was penniless put him in a violent situation, since he could not even sit down to order the most modest and cheapest drink that was served in the gambling den.

From the door I peek for the unmistakable silhouette of Phelps. He could not locate him and this forced him to start a gesture of disgust.

But instead, deep down, he discovered the gambler. He could be unmistakably located, not only because of his sharp personality, but because sitting on a towering stool to dominate the long table he rose almost a meter above the general level of points.

But Cosimo didn't see him. He was very attentive to the game and at that time, for him there was no other world than the roulette wheel and the long racket with which he swept the cloth.

Tyson dared to go ahead and take a walk around as if looking for a table. He absentmindedly examined everything within reach of his hand, and thus his eyes were fixed with preference on the half dozen girls who served as a distraction to the miners and other customers to animate the dance.

And among all of them, a relatively thin blond girl, but with very feminine forms, who danced with a well-dressed individual and even a good dancer, caught his attention in a particular way. They were an excellent couple and he did not know if this was what forced him to focus on the girl in preference.

Tyson guessed that he would be around his age. He had shiny blond hair, gracefully coiffed. Her blue eyes were candid and melancholic, her complexion rosy, and her lips thin and well-traced.

In contrast to the rest of her peers, she did not need to resort to flashy outfits to make herself stand out. Quite the contrary, she was honestly wearing a pale blue blouse closed to the neck, an ankle-length black skirt, and mid-heeled shoes of the same color.

Yet there was something special about her distinguished bearing and her serene, graceful figure that made her powerfully attractive.

Tyson gawked at her as she danced next to him and told himself that this was the type of woman he had always liked, although this one, from the environment in which she was struggling, did not seem to possess the total qualities of his preference.

But his silent contemplation ceased when he discovered Grant who had just emerged from a back door in the packaging of a prince surrounded by his court.

Phelps walked across the room spreading smiles and greetings, and Tyson, overcoming his shyness, started walking to cut him off and approach him with his request.

"Please, Mr. Phelps! "He murmured." Would you be so kind as to attend me for a moment?

The aforementioned measured him up and down with his sharp gaze. The humble aspect of his interlocutor and his battered attire did not predispose him in his favor and with an evasive gesture he replied:

"Boy, here it is not customary to beg.

Tyson blushed and half choking stammered:

"I'm not begging, sir.

"Well then, what do you want?

"Ask for something, but noble. I'm here without a job and without a penny. I had not put anything in my mouth for two days and if I had dinner tonight it was because of the kindness of a generous man who, knowing my hunger, invited me to satisfy him. I just wanted to ask you for a job. You have a good business, you will need people for certain tasks, washing dishes, splitting wood, I don't know, something to justify a salary and I wanted to beg you to provide me with something to earn even to eat. Do you think it is too much to ask you to have plenty of everything?

Grant looked at him coldly and said:

"And are you not ashamed to ask for a job of that base here, when you are a young, strong man with the conditions to live on something more productive?

"I do not know what; tell me.

"I don't think it's accurate. Those jobs that you ask for remain for the old and useless beings. Young men who lower themselves in such a degrading way have nothing to do in an environment like this. Here you come to earn money by whatever means and when you are young and determined, you always find a way to live relatively well with a little daring and a little less than scruples. You're only a few miles from Tombstone, Arizona's harshest mining center, and not in a squishy eastern town. Don't you realize that?

"What do you propose to me, to make me a robber?

"I do not propose anything to you, I show you a path and I warn you so that you realize that you have come wrong. If you don't feel like doing more than what you ask for, the best thing to do is take the path and head north.

Tyson was disappointed and angry at the same time. This rogue judged everyone by the same standard and took pleasure in pushing men towards evil. Hurrying his patience he insisted:

"Excuse me; everyone has a concept of their life. I only want to work, even if only modestly, could you not grant me such a job? If you reserve it for older men, a young man will always make you more useful.

Grant, pushing him gently toward the door, replied:

"Do not insist. I feel sorry for such miserable and absurd aspirations. Think of my advice that is worth more than such a job.

But Tyson, desperate, was reluctant to leave without trying to move him.

"Please," he insisted, "even if it's for the smallest thing there is, but give me something.

Phelps angrily growled:

"Enough, stupid. I told you I don't need you.

With a terrible push he threw him against the revolving door with which he collided, being thrown backwards.

At that moment, two tall, strong guys, between thirty and thirty-five years of age, were about to push open the revolving door to enter the establishment. Both were modestly dressed in plaid shirts, blue denim pants, and high leather boots. Their flexible waists were girded by the wide belt from which the heavy colts hung, and their heads touched with the wide pearl gray cowboy hat with wide brims and dented crown.

When they wanted to realize what was happening on the other side of the door, Tyson's body fell backward on them and the rough arms of the two visitors served as bumpers to prevent him from hitting their backs in the dust of the road.

One of them commented sarcastically:

"Youngster; here people tend to go out of their way to avoid bumping into anyone. Going out on your back is too dangerous; especially if you run into men who are less calm than us.

Tyson, confused and pale, stammered:

"Excuse me; I did not do it of my own free will. It was that pig Grant who unexpectedly threw me like this.

"Ah come on! It was Phelps's doing. What did you do to him?

Ask him for work.

"What do you say, boy? Do I work Grant?

"Yes, I was desperate and without food for two days and I dared to ask him for something to earn a living. A square of dishwasher, to cut firewood, whatever. He made fun of me and recommended that I become a robber who is more productive. As I insisted, he threw me this way.

The two newcomers looked at each other and seemed to understand each other with that gesture because one of them commented:

"You can't expect anything else from Grant. Since he didn't make his money by preaching, he believes there are no more practical ways to earn it.

And turning to look at his companion, he asked:

"What do we do with him, Corny?

"Whatever you like, Caleb.

"Well, boy, you say you haven't eaten for two days ...

"This night Yes. I hadn't eaten for two days and tonight, when I was desperately prodding a piece of meat with a branch through the mesh of a shop window, a kind man discovered me and invited me to dinner. It had been a long time since I put that much into my body, but tomorrow ...

"You say there was a man who did that to you? There is only one here capable of such genius. I bet it was Cosimo Lamore.

"Yes, gentlemen, the same and he promised to help me if he could.

"Well boy, what's your name?

"Tyson Winslow.

"Well then, Tyson, you can join us for now. We do not eat delicacies, sometimes we do not even know if we are going to eat something, but in the end we solve the problem and there will always be something for everyone. Hunger, divided between three, is less than between two, because it touches less. We've already had dinner tonight and we even have some money for a pint of beer. It happens with us.

"You are very kind, but I do not want to burden your savings with unnecessary expenses on my part. I thank you ...

"Shut up, Tyson. Our expenses are never superfluous, because man needs to eat, drink, play, have fun, and while he needs it, whatever he spends on it is necessary.

And they gently pushed him saying:

"Come on, boy, go ahead.

Tyson, prompted by the pleasant reception of this strange couple, obeyed and pushed the door past the two men, while they delayed a moment to make a quick consultation.

Grant, not far from the front door, seeing the boy in the establishment again, hardened the features of his face and advancing towards him, roared:

"Haven't I kicked you out of here, louse? Get out right now if you don't want me to kick you out.

And she threw herself on him, grasping him by the knot of the handkerchief, pushing him to throw him again.

But at that moment the two cowboys, if they were, were entering after the young man and, observing Grant's attitude, the so-called Corny grabbed the angry Phelps by the arm and squeezing him with enough force coldly ordered:

"Quieto comes with us.

Grant understood that the order vexed him and made him look ridiculous in the eyes of the people and trying to evade the order he growled:

"I have thrown him out of here and ...

"Enough, Grant," Caleb warned sharply. " This is a public establishment and there is room for everyone who comes to spend money. I have said that he comes in our company and that is enough.

The gambler tensed his muscles and his arm began to incline slightly toward his waist, but the movement was light and instantly rectified. The two men, even lighter than he, already had their hands on their hips.

"Is there anything to oppose my words? Caleb asked mockingly.

Grant, trying to hide his anger, replied:

"If it is backed by someone with a guarantee, nothing.

"Agree. Come on, boy, there is a table left unoccupied; get us three whiskeys.

Phelps turned and the three of them hurried to the table. Tyson, who had followed the entire phase of the dialogue with eager interest, murmured:

"I don't like the way you looked at them, gentlemen. I would be sorry if they had a dislike for him for me.

"Don't worry about it, boy. Here you have dislikes for contemplating the moon. Grant will do very well to take care of the business and not look for dangerous complications, because quite a few come his way without looking for them.

The whiskey was served. Tyson was staring at it with fear, for it was a drink he had rarely tasted and knew of its powerful effects on men like him who were not hardened to bear it.

But he did not dare to confess his weakness or to make them despise to reject it and he prepared to go down it in small gulps.

Corny, calmly lighting his pipe, exclaimed:

"Well boy, get your story out. At least we know who we are going to alternate with.

Tyson gave them a short and concise account of his life and the ordeal he had endured, culminating the story with the unpleasant dialogue he had just had with Grant.

"This guy was always like this. He does not conceive of anyone less a rogue than himself and if he bumps into someone who is not, he feels envy or contempt. Well, putting that aside you don't seem to be of much use, buddy.

"Depending on what it is," he replied timidly.

"I mean what here is called serving for something.

"If you mean what Grant told me, I certainly won't do it.

"You could be used for something similar, but in the opposite direction.

"I do not understand them.

"I will explain myself. Here only men are needed in the exact sense of the word. If some are dedicated to evil and others to good, that is already apart. In a corrupt society, evil must be attacked with something more than good intentions and it takes men as tough as the opposite to get out of their way. Undesirables are galore here, what some are looking for are the ones on the opposite side and from that ... there was some very bad seed this year in Southeast Arizona.

"Are you referring to authorities?

"No, when the authority makes its appearance here with some efficiency, the cemeteries will have to be emptied beforehand to fill them again.

"Then...

"But there are certain individuals who need the help of brave men and with a certain decency to protect their interests in the absence of authorities and organizations that defend them. For example, we know of a certain mining company that has started to pile up silver extracted from the mines and needs to supply it. You have to move it to Tucson and other safe centers to lock it in the boxes of the banks and this is the problem. While the amount stored is not very tempting, they can defend it with relative guarantees against an assault, but when it is large, its permanence here is dangerous and to send it to the good of God, even more dangerous. For that they need brave men, capable of feeling no more selfishness than receiving a good pay to guard and protect that deposit and that is a means like any other of earning a good pay to live well without the need to resort to robbery and assault, but here people are attacked by greed in the highest degree and prefers the chance of an assault, not knowing if it is going to go well or badly and it is going to make money, to settle for a decent and safe allowance. I hope you understand me.

"Yes, I'm beginning to understand him," Tyson replied, interested in the words of his makeshift partner. You try to recruit honest men to protect those shipments that must leave the basin at any moment.

"You have spoken like a wise man," Corny stated.

"And you are going to commit to doing that.

"We are trying to be in a position to commit ourselves, which is not the same. We urgently need to resolve this issue, because our economic possibilities are very scarce and things are urgent. It all depends on whether we form enough numbers for it.

"Yes, and they propose to put myself at your service.

"We had thought that you might be of use to it. Of course we do not give you the absolute category to judge you an outstanding element, but ... if you have courage, if you really want an honest job where you can earn to live well and you are willing to do whatever is necessary to achieve it, then maybe we can do something for you.

Tyson, after thinking excitedly for a few minutes, replied:

"I have never considered myself a coward, although this environment is too dense for me and I feel cowering in it. My handling of a weapon is very poor, but I would do everything in my power to justify my pay if they felt that I could even be used to drive a cart with the silver. After all, a driver, they will need and I understand a lot about that. What I could do afterwards in a desperate case I cannot guarantee.

Caleb, smiling sympathetically, replied:

"That's how they talk, boy, and I've always had more confidence in those who have judged themselves less valuable than they think they are, than in those who have bragged a lot and when push comes to shove have not lived up to their bravado. You say well; a silver conductor will always be precise and in the absence of something better you could take care of it. Well, at the moment we cannot speak more about this matter because there are enough details missing, but it is already something. While things are sorting out, we take you on our own and at least three better or worse meals a day will not be lacking. That way you won't have to beg guys like that rogue for work, and you won't be forced to poke a stick into the meat to find out what it tastes like.

"Oh!" Tyson exclaimed gratefully. " You do not know that what you are proposing is something so valuable to me that I have to bless the moment when it occurred to me to come to this den to apply for a job of that type. I think if I had a revolver handy, right now I would shoot him right where he is.

He spoke exalted. Little by little the whiskey disappeared from his glass and the strength of the alcohol was beginning to take its toll on him.

Caleb, smiling, replied:

"Don't get hot, boy. That piece is too big for you to collect, but ... maybe you will have the pleasure of watching someone else fill his belly with lead. And now that we agree, we are going to celebrate the meeting having fun for a while. It is danced here and these girls are quite nice. Do not waste time and pair with one.

In order for the pianist to take a well-deserved rest, the piano had been muted and the girls were fluttering around the premises from table to table, called and invited by some of the clients.

Tyson, hearing Caleb's invitation, had turned his head, instinctively searching for the graceful silhouette of the blonde girl, who had caught his attention so much.

Now, a little excited by the whiskey, he was more attracted to her and a mad desire to dance with the young woman had taken hold of him.

Corny noted the strange glint in her gaze and the direction it was leading and smiled, nudging his partner. Then I comment:

"Do you like it, boy?

"Very much, I don't deny it.

"You don't have bad taste. There are many here who admire the girl, but Betty, "the Blonde", is an exquisite but difficult snack for many palates. Oddly enough, it must be admitted that she is a decent girl, who was thrown onto this dirty beach by the onslaught of life like a broken ship. It takes arrests to know how to stand firm among this leprosy that surrounds her, although ... perhaps it has served as a shield in some part that Grant ...

When Corny did not conclude the comment, Tyson, exalted, exclaimed:

" What do you mean?

"Nothing concrete. Grant is infatuated with Betty, even though she forces him to settle for platonic adoration. It pays her well, she watches over her like a tiger and this forces many to watch what they do about her. After all, Betty is not stupid and knows how to take advantage of this dangerous situation.

"But…, being that way they say, why doesn't he go away?

" Where to? Maybe in Tombstone they would pay her better in some place, but what about the danger that she would run alone and with no one to watch her back?

"Anyway, you could leave this hell and go to the East.

"She will know why you don't. You don't always get what you want in life.

Caleb got up, saying:

"Let's dance. There is Carole who is beckoning me. Come on, boy, go ahead and if you like Betty, ask her to dance. It is her mission and she is obliged not to refuse.

Tyson did not hesitate, and encouraged by that strange failure that burned in his veins, he went straight to Betty, inviting her to dance.

The girl, indifferent, did not refuse, and he gently embraced her waist, to launch himself into the delights of the dance.

Corny, a little tense, exclaimed:

"Caleb, you were wrong to put the boy in this hornet's nest. After what has happened, I'm afraid Grant won't be too happy with me dancing with Betty and doing some humiliating rudeness with him. The boy is not ripe for these drinks.

"Maybe, but you have to train him. Let's see what happens, and if things got too sour for him, what would we paint but you and me here?

"Well. Anyway, I think one day we will stumble upon him. Grant is more than just a gambling den operator, and someday evidence will emerge against him.

Meanwhile, Tyson danced with the blonde and seemed to forget everything around him.

But Grant had realized the mischief devised by the two friends, and as Tyson danced with Betty, he lost control of his nerves and, advancing impetuously between the groups of clients who were blocking his way, he reached the couple and clutching By the arm of the young man, he pulled him violently and although Tyson tried to keep his balance when he released his partner, he could not prevent himself from being thrown by the savage pull, falling to the ground.

But Grant, beside himself, leaned over Tyson and grabbed his neck, bellowed:

"Get out of here, you filthy beggar! Get out of here, I tell you, if you don't want me to drag you out! You are too lousy to allow you to dance with Betty.

Tyson gritted his teeth furiously. He felt attacked and the fact that they put him in such a violent and ridiculous situation, subjecting him to curiosity and perhaps the mockery of dozens of eyes, fired his blood even more. He had hated the presumptuous gambler from the start, and this hatred culminated in the threat he had just thrown at him.

And revolting recklessly against him, he bellowed:

"Hey, she's here for that and don't make those threats at me, because ...

Betty, who had reacted, because she knew Grant very well, tried to prevent a very unequal fight and wanted to get between them, but in doing so, Phelps, who had thrown himself impetuously against the young man, found no other way to divert her from his path than raising his arm and dropping his hand on the girl's face, who emitted a howl as if she had been bitten by a rattlesnake.

The cowardly action of the gambler was the last spur for Tyson, who, in a savage way, jumped on Grant and before he had time to raise his arm again, he received a fierce punch on the chin and grotesquely rolled on the floor of the premises. like a strange toad.

That was superior to his endurance and, rising as quickly as possible, he let his eyes reflect all the evil and cruelty that he was capable of and put a hand to his side to draw the revolver and shoot at that unexpected enemy, who, without a weapon some at the waist, there was nothing he could do to avoid being shot through.

But in an unexpected way, two arms emerged with two "Colts" at the sides of the gambler and Corny's cold voice warning:

"Watch out, Grant, that man has no weapons other than his fists to defend himself and with them he has attacked him. If you are not able to answer with the same weapons, go into a corner like the rats, but do not appeal to cowardly murder. When you show off as a man, you have to prove it.

Phelps's face had twisted into a rude grin. His eyes were like burning coals and his lips were livid with anger. He glared at Corny and bellowed:

"Corny, stop meddling in things you don't care about. You are making a lot of mistakes and may have to regret them if you give yourself time to do so.

"Possibly, if all the guys I have to run into are as devious as you are. But take good care of your health in case these threats turn out to be expensive ... I have long known about you much more than you suppose and I have not forgotten it. This is a sincere warning, because when I say that I do not forget a person, it is to keep them present in my few prayers.

The gambler stiffened, and then turning to Tyson, who was as pale as a dead man, he yelled:

Get out of Fairbank soon, you lousy indecent; Get out of here, because where I find you again I will kill you like a poisonous snake.

"Do it soon, if you can," cried Tyson, "because if not ..., the day that I am able to handle a revolver moderately, I will look for you without waiting for you to look for me and I will blow your head off, so that you do not be so cowardly again, slapping a defenseless woman. You are the most despicable creature on earth.

Phelps made terrible efforts not to draw his revolver at the threat of the two cowboys, but there was a hunger to kill in his ophidian eyes. Caleb ended the dramatic situation, ordering:

"Tyson, come out ahead. Go!

The young man doubted. He was not very satisfied with this ending, although he half understood that it had been the luckiest for him, due to the intervention of his two improvised friends, but Caleb's sharp command seemed to exert fascination on him and he slowly crossed the room with direction to the door, followed by the gaze of all the customers, who had been silent witnesses to the tragic incident.

Due to the effects of the event, the game had been interrupted and Cosimo, from his high seat, had witnessed it all.

A strange smile was wandering on his bloodless lips the whole time, as if that scene had been for him one of the funniest spectacles in the world.

Corny and Caleb watched the boy's exit without losing sight of the owner of the joint, and when they considered him safe, they prepared to imitate him.

But before leaving, Caleb coldly warned:

"Grant, gambling is knowing how to lose. Forget this and don't worry about the boy anymore. It is loyal advice that I give you, even if you do not deserve it.

"I give you another one, Caleb. Go to Tombstone and don't show up around here anymore. Maybe they will earn more from it.

"Thanks. Until tomorrow, we'll be back here for another fun time.

And with this derogatory reply, he left the gambling den, followed by his partner.

On the road, Tyson joined them. The night air had somewhat cooled the boy's heated head and he was beginning to realize the danger he had been in and the strained situation in which he had placed his two generous friends.

And humbly apologizing, he pleaded:

"Forgive me. I didn't know what he was doing, but that guy treated me in a humiliating way and then ... you see ... he slapped that poor girl. A man, no matter how cowardly he may be, cannot stand idly by when he beholds such cowardice.

"Let's not talk about that anymore, Tyson" stated Caleb patting him on the back. You were a bit reckless when challenging a man with a revolver at his side, but you have behaved with dignity.

"I didn't think I would do that. I expected him to react and admit the fight.

"He is afraid that they will make him uglier than he is and he will never accept exposing himself to having his face pounded. It was more comfortable and expeditious what I tried. Well, now you have to be careful just in case. Where do you have your lair?

"In nowhere. I have slept two nights in the open air, but today Lamore had put two dollars in my pocket to look for an inn.

"You will sleep in our apartment. Where two fit, three are tightened. Go!

And they went to one of the two inns in the town.

* * *

With the absence of Tyson and the two cowboys, calm seemed to have been reborn in the joint. Grant, pale with courage and accusing the trace of the terrible punch that the young man administered to him, did not know how to vent his fury and turning to Betty, who, cornered at one end of the room, looked like a marble statue so white and hermetic, bellowed:

"You are to blame, you coquette pig. You are playing with me like the cat plays with the mouse and you forget that my power is so strong, that I could crush you like an ant. You have abused the fact that I have a certain inclination for you, but if you think that this will serve to create annoying situations for me, you are wrong, because then I will forget what attracts me and I will only see in you one of many that have passed through my hands.

Betty, in a colorless voice, replied:

"You are obnoxious, Grant, and also incomprehensible. I have a contract with you that binds me and I am a slave to my commitments, but not to the extent of being overwhelmed in that way. My obligation is to serve your customers without distinction and I did nothing but fulfill it. If he had warned me not to dance with him, I would have refused, because I neither know him nor care about anything, but, after all, he has been more noble than you, because he has even shown that you have the courage to stand up for him. a battered woman, while you ...

"Do you want to shut up, toad in skirts? That guy is an idiot classifying women of your ilk.

Betty, as if whipped by a whip, stood up screaming:

"Enough ...! What do you have to say about me? I am a woman as decent as it is unfortunate, since fate threw me here to bear her rudeness.

" Decent? Well, at least you brag about it. Here you are only one of several hired to amuse the mob, and that guy is an idiot creating dangers for defending the lowest that is between us.

The insult ignited the girl's anger and, reaching for a heavy glass on the nearest table, she threw it angrily at Grant's head. His speed, avoiding the strange projectile, prevented him from receiving it in the full forehead.

But that was too much for him to bear. After being beaten by Tyson, he could not ignore that a woman and more a slave in his service, also attacked him by throwing a glass at her face and like a tiger he jumped on her ready to mistreat her, but a fine and dapper hand, it emerged in time, holding her arm in the air. The pressure, though it seemed gentle, gave him the impression of a pincer viciously clinging to his flesh.

He scrambled to confront Cosimo Lamore, who coldly and serenely warned:

"Okay now, Grant. A man should not do that.

"Go to hell, Lamore, and stay where no one calls you. You are just a gambler here at my service and nothing more.

"Only there" indicated Cosimo, pointing to the gaming table where another carved in his position. Here I am a man like any other and do not say that I work for you, because that is independent. It is true that I am a gambler, but you are not the one to hold it against me.

"Are you also going to come out in defense of that dead mosquito? Do you suppose that for her I am going to let myself be overwhelmed and put in evidence? Don't think so.

"It was not her, but you, with your intemperance. Betty fulfilled her obligation, and if you had something against the boy, you should have solved it alone ... and in a way more in keeping with what you presume. He was able to assassinate him with impunity and I don't think that would have added much glory to his fame.

"Why didn't you bring a revolver like any other?

"Perhaps because whoever is starving, if they don't have enough to eat, they should have less to acquire a weapon. Perhaps it could also be because he does not know how to handle it.

"So, do not take refuge in not wearing a revolver to guarantee your life. He who does not have the guts to defend his person in these latitudes, do not come.

"It is possible, but listen to one thing. I think you would be wrong to look down on that boy. Guns or no guns, he has shown he is fearless and ... I may be wrong, but if you have time and learn to handle a revolver, beware of him, Grant, because he will not be despised.

" That? Well, don't make me laugh, Lamore. You won't be the one to see him spitting lead out of a Colt's barrel eye.

"It will be because I have little life left, if not ... who knows. And now, calm down and don't be stupid. Come on, Betty, compose yourself too and forget about this unpleasant incident. When the nerves are unleashed, a lot of nonsense is committed that sometimes weighs heavily. I learned it in practice and it served me as a lesson.

"Well, we'll talk about that. Many things have happened that undermine the discipline of the premises and have created a slighted situation for me. Women always have to be the magic stone where one has to stumble when least expected.

"It will be because you have wanted it.

"Because she wanted it. You know ... well, let's not talk about this any more for the moment!

The incident seemed settled and normal activity reigned in the gambling den, but Betty, devastated with nerves and with a terrible desire to break down in tears, seemed an automaton moving through the premises, not by its own will, but by a superior force that drove her to follow the routine of her life.

More at dawn, when the place began to be empty and the young woman went to the small room where she had her street clothes, her nerves loosened as if they had just released their ties and, dropping on a seat, broke into bitterness sobs.

Cosimo, who had not lost sight of her, perhaps guessing how the girl's nervous breakdown would end, pushed the, half-closed door of the tabuco and, approaching her, placed his thin hand on the hair of the troubled young woman and with a paternal accent. , He said:

"Come on Betty, be strong and calm down. You are a woman of mettle and you should not let yourself be overcome by these things typical of here. Come on, pick up your clothes and let's go. I will accompany you to your accommodation.

And she meekly obeyed, leaving the gambling den in the company of the gambler.

The night was wonderful. In the deep blue sky, the stars shone like scattered diamonds, and the air was soft and caressing. The road was deserted and all was silence and gloom.

They started walking slowly. Lamore had his pipe burning and did not dare to break the silence that seized the girl's mind, until, being several steps ahead, he leaned against a wall and cried out with terrible despair:

"I would like to go to bed tonight and never see the light of day again.

Come on, Betty, don't be pessimistic. Life has many setbacks and ...

"Life will have many setbacks for some, for me it is such a heavy burden and without any moment of relief, that I would gain more by ending it.

"Do not say that. You are very young and you still do not know what the future may have in store for you. Like your cross, many of us carry it on our shoulders and because we have left the best of our existence behind, we can no longer wait for everything to change and reserve some compensation for us.

But for youth, there is always a point of hope.

"What do you know about my cross, Mr. Lamore?

"Nothing, indeed, girl, as you do not know anything about the others. I am too discreet a man to ask questions when no one anticipates confiding in me. I have known you for three months that you have been here and you have been such a reserved woman that you never opened your mouth to cast out something of your yesterday. I do not blame you, because letting off steam with certain elements pulling out thorns that hurt one's soul is as much as throwing flowers to pigs. Sometimes instead of finding consolation for our sorrows with these sentimental confidences, what we achieve is to serve as a mockery to people.

"You said so, Mr. Lamore. Of course not everyone is like you. I have also wondered how and why you have come to stop here.

He interrupted her with a gesture, saying:

"That same question I have asked myself about you. Men are such a vulgar product that our excesses justify finding ourselves in any environment, no matter how harsh and exotic it may be, but you ...

"Same. Do you not appreciate it that way seeing how these places in the West are populated with wretches who ...?

"Wait a minute, Betty. We agree in part on that. There are many women, girls who rolled down the paths of life and will no longer be able to get up. They all belong to the same lot. You, on the other hand, are still very far from that. I am not a fortune-teller, but I am a bit of a psychologist, and I am not mistaken in stating that, fortunately for you, despite everything, you are in a position to throw yourself off that path and dust yourself off the road without knowing you are stained by it.

"Why can you say so? I have a hard time admitting that you are the only man capable of believing in me.

"It will be because I am the only man who, looking like those around me, I am intimately different.

"I think that is the reason" said the young woman trying to find his eyes in the dark. If you knew ...

"I don't want to know anything, girl, if you don't have the need to vent and you think I am worthy of knowing your secrets in case I can help you carry your cross.

"Oh, I'm sure you are the only man to whom I can make a confession!

"At least, he will be one of the few that I will understand and forget later.

"Thank you, but don't think there is something shameful in my life that makes me blush, at least as far as I am personally concerned.

"I'm sure it is, Betty.

Thank you for your good opinion. Today I feel so fatigued and anguished that I don't have the courage to tell you about my eventful life, but one day, not taking long, it will be a comfort for me to vent to someone and no one better than you. My wish right now is to dream that one day I will fulfill my contract with that beast Grant and gather enough to leave this hell and march far away from here, forgetting everything around me.

"It will be the best you can do, girl, and if I can help you in anything, you can count on me. I am not rich, none of us are in this environment, except those who, like Grant, exploit others, but I have something that is available to you at some point if you need it.

"Thanks.

They had reached the girl's quarters. She offered her hand to the gambler and he kissed her forehead gently. Then they parted ways.

Three days passed without any new incident disturbing the somewhat scandalous and fictitious peace of the gambling den.

Betty, in an effort of will, had collected herself by resuming her mission on the premises. Grave, tight, tense, she kept her promise, and in all that time Grant had never spoken to her again.

Lamore, as soft and enigmatic as ever, carried out his duties at the gaming table, seemingly indifferent to his surroundings, but he kept watching both the girl and the irascible Phelps. He sensed that this truce was only apparent and that one day a new conflict would arise that would break it.

Because the gambler had studied Grant thoroughly and also knew him to be a conceited and arrogant man.

Perhaps against his will he had become infatuated with Betty and for him it was an unbearable bitterness to stumble upon the impregnable barrier of her revulsion.

As for Grant, he had a lot on his hands that worried him too much, and under these circumstances, he seemed to have relegated this annoying matter to second place. He hadn't seen Tyson and his two rough companions since, and this helped to keep him calm around him.

He received many visits from highly significant elements; he exchanged brief conversations in a low voice with certain clients and, sometimes, he would take someone to his small office and mysteriously lock himself up with him, without anyone being able to guess what he had been talking about.

One night days later, when the bustle in the joint had stopped and the staff were preparing to gather everything to close, a tall and wiry man, with a striking and haughty appearance, arrived and made an expressive gesture to Grant. The latter gestured for him to enter the back part reserved as an office and after ordering that once the premises were in order, they closed, he went inside.

The office was relatively small and not badly furnished. Business demands that demanded more space for exploitation had greatly compressed the space and a long and narrow strip had been reserved for the entire back of the house, divided into two halves. The one on the left was destined for an office and on the other side he had built three tabucos so that the girls could change their clothes for their work.

Phelps came in with a bottle of whiskey and two glasses, and after setting them on the table and closing the door from the inside, he asked:

"What news do you bring, Sttup?

He took the bottle, poured himself a good glass and after draining it with relish, he fell on one of the seats, affirming:

"I think I got some good news, Grant.

"That is good for everyone. Speaks.

"I will confess that I have had a bit of luck and that has made things easier. But apart from this, the thing is well worth it.

"I'll start by telling you that if these jeans are really such cowboys, they are more difficult to monitor and surprise than you thought. They live in perpetual alarm and you have to walk with lead feet to be jealous of them without them noticing anything. Two days ago I followed them to Tombstone, where I saw them enter the Esperanza mine, which, as you know, is so far the best organized and exploited mine. It was hard for me to admit that they were going to ask for a position as excavators, and I assumed that the visit was due to something more intriguing.

»They spent more than an hour in the engineer and the manager's office and then, accompanied by the latter, who was patting them goodbye on the back, they left the village and returned here.

»For three nights I have seen the three of them move from one place to another, visiting taverns and grocery stores and talking to some elements with whom I have no dealings, since they do not belong to our circle of friends; therefore, it was not easy to be able to know a word of what they spoke with such subjects.

"But chance has led them to contact Groyn Brandon, a fellow with the air of a preacher whom I have secretly employed at some time and whom they have seen very few times in my company and it has been he who has me. put on the track.

Taking you for one of the few unsuspicious elements at Fairbank, he has made you a proposition. The one to accept a contract for several days with a fairly decent pay, to join them and drive to Tucson a cart loaded with silver bars that the operators of the Esperanza mine need to send to the Bank of the town to decongest the deposit of the mine and to prevent someone, attracted by the value of what is already stored, from attempting a coup against it.

"From the little that Brandon has been told, we know that one day, not yet fixed, the wagon will leave Tombstone one morning, apparently laden with straw seines, to mislead. The straw will only cover the external part to hide the true content and according to their suspicions, six men will be in charge of driving, guarding and defending the merchandise.

Two of them, of course, will be Corny and Caleb; the other, that young guy who has joined them, and the fourth, my friend Brandon, who has already agreed to join them. Of the other two who must make up the party, he does not know a word, but hopes to find out before setting out.

This is the matter. As you will understand, the cargo is worth risking and, knowing the main thing, what it contains and the number of men who have to defend it, we have enough to organize the coup, counting on my friend Brandon at the critical moment. they will stand by our side and it will be a tragic wedge embedded within themselves.

And now that you know what there is, you will decide what to do.

Grant's slimy eyes gleamed as if fever set them on fire. Filling his glass with a slightly trembling pulse, he said:

"I knew this had to come since I decided to settle here. You can't eat silver and you have to get it out of the mines, but in the case of such an unsafe place, as long as there is no real organization here and they appoint a body of watchmen of the basin, they will have to resort to similar tricks to try their luck. .

"I don't trust that we can deliver many blows, but by successfully completing two or three good ones, we will have gotten enough not to worry about the future. I have everything well planned and the money will mysteriously disappear for the moment, and then leave here in doses and through safe channels, without anyone suspecting anything.

And this news makes me doubly happy, because in addition to helping us to strike a good blow, it will serve me particularly to take revenge on those three guys, making them disappear when they least expect it and without them suspecting which shadowy hand has pulled the strings to dispatch them hell. I promise you a good part in this first job, if with the shipment we eliminate those guys.

"So stay in touch with Brandon and I'll set up everything else. We will give those six guys nine and as we will also enjoy Brandon's help and with the surprise factor, you will practically be ten against five and that is enough.

"In due course I will tell you who will be the men that I will place at your command for the matter and the place where they will fight. We can only know this when your friend tells us for sure when the wagon will leave and what the departure itinerary is. And since no more can be discussed on this matter, we will drop it and when the time comes we will launch the attack.

They refilled their glasses toasting the success of the dirty business and Sttup left the office. When Grant came out of the room accompanying his partner, the waiters were finishing their collection.

"Is there nothing else or no one left?

"No, boss. The last ones to come out were Lamore, who left a quarter of an hour ago, and Betty, who left a few moments ago.

"Okay, close up and leave.

Grant took all the money collected from the bar drawer and went to the office, where in a steel box he kept the money along with the money he had already received from the gaming tables. Then, by a narrow staircase at the back, he ascended to his rooms, installed in the upper part of the gambling den.

He had never been so satisfied as that night. He was going to do a magnificent business and at the same time to take revenge for the threats and injuries of his three enemies.

* * *

Lamore, the gambler, lived in a small building almost on the outskirts of town. It was one of the modest old houses in Fairbank, before it became a more modern and rough town, and the owner was the widow of a farm boy, who had had the misfortune to put his head within reach of the Hind leg of a sluggish mule and, therefore, when he wanted to realize his recklessness, his shoe was stuck in his brains.

The widow had reserved a small but clean room for him. The cot with the corn-straw mattress, a footstool, and a chest were the only pieces of furniture he had. It also had a washbasin and a brass jug that he filled with water on the door when he got up.

When he arrived at his lodging almost at dawn, as was his custom, he did not go to bed immediately. Before doing so, he would sit on the edge of the cot, light his pipe, and indulge in thoughts that he only knew by the zeal with which he guarded them.

That night, like some others, he opened the chest to take out a clean shirt. Just as he carefully brushed and arranged his outer clothing on the crude coat rack that had been nailed to the wall, so he used to change his shirt almost every day. He was a clean and dapper man, who did not allow himself to be overcome by dirt and neglect like many others.

After removing the shirt and preparing it for the moment to rise, he stood tense in front of the chest, regarding him with a frown and a gesture of indecision, as if tormented by a doubt.

And then, suddenly, he leaned over, picked up some garments that covered the entire opening, and from the bottom he took out a small carved wooden box, the lid of which he gently lifted. From the bottom he produced a gold medallion that contained the faded portrait of a beautiful woman. Although the action of time had printed a gray patina on the portrait, one could still admire the beauty of that woman, who must have been a splendid blonde, with an angelic face that appreciated the sad air of her clear eyes, possibly blue.

Cosimo kissed the portrait with emotion and placed it back on the bottom of the box, then produced the portrait of a slender, virile-looking, attractive man. The portrayed man wore a typical hunter's outfit and, judging by his clothing, he must have been hunting bison and bears. On his shoulder he wore a double-barreled rifle and at his belt a formidable hunting knife. There was no more in the box. Lamore put the portraits together and muttered:

I'm sorry, my dear. Luck never accompanied me and it was not possible for me to take revenge. The West is so great that it does not seem as easy as some believe to find a specific man in it. I suspect that I will go down to the tomb without being able to fulfill the oath I made you. "

And he put the box in the bottom of the chest, preparing to get into bed.

But suddenly someone banged on the door. Lamore, intrigued, wondered who could call at such hours of the morning and just in case, putting the small revolver in his pocket and, with his hand in it, he opened the bedroom door and went out into the corridor to cross him to be the one who opened it. the door.

Before doing so, he asked discreetly:

"Who goes?

He shuddered with anguish hurrying to open it, when he caught the trembling and anguished voice of Betty, who pleaded:

"It's me, Mr. Lamore. Me what...

He took her by the arm, dragging her inside, not without glancing outside in case someone was chasing her and then excitedly asked:

"Betty, please speak up! What happens?

"Oh, something terrible! Well, not exactly me, but something monstrous, infamous, cowardly ... I didn't know what to do and rushed to come looking for him. I don't know maybe I've done something stupid.

" Because? When you have decided to do it, some special reason will have forced you. Come on, come in and talk.

And he led her to his modest bedroom, forcing her to sit on the edge of the bed.

" What happened? I left you just half an hour ago and ...

"It was something terrible, which I found out by chance and since I did not know what to do, I have come to tell you, because you are the only decent man I deal with.

"Thanks for the compliment, but whatever counts.

"I found out by chance, Mr. Lamore. You had already left and I was the last of all in the small apartment where I keep my clothes.

As I think you are well aware, the wooden wall of it separates Grant's office. Sometimes while I was dressing I would hear him stirring in it, but I never gave any importance to this fact.

But tonight, something unusual has happened. While I was changing my suit in silence, I caught a rumor of conversation on the other side of the partition and it surprised me that, at such hours, Grant had a visitor and without being able to avoid it, I was tempted to know who it was, what they were talking about and apply the ear to the septum.

And I heard something terrible, Mr. Lamore. The visitor was Donald Sttup, you know who the guy is; and they were talking about something that affected the boy from the other night and his two friends.

But there was still more. Plans were being made for an attack on a silver convoy, which will leave Tombstone one of these nights and will be protected by these three brave men.

Lamore, amazed, asked:

"What do you say, Betty?

"What you hear; I swear.

"Speaks. Tell me every detail without forgetting anything.

The girl, nervous, repeated word for word everything she had heard and when she finished the story, she added:

"Please, Mr. Lamore, something must be done to prevent this assault and above all, to assassinate those decent men with impunity! They have unsuspectingly brought the traitor Brandon into their midst and are in dire danger.

"Well, girl, don't blame yourself for so little.

"Little do you say?

"I mean that nothing irremediable has happened yet and that everything can be solved. The thing apparently is still in embryo and in the time that remains, many things can be tried to frustrate it.

"But I can not do anything. A woman...

"No one asks you for it, little girl. You've done enough to uncover the scoundrel and report it to me. The rest will be my responsibility.

"Are you really interested in avoiding it?

"You can be sure that I will.

And what will he do?

"I'll tell you when the time comes, because I have to study it. You have to be careful so that Grant does not suspect anything, particularly of you and that requires some thought, but I promise you that they will not commit such villainy.

"Thanks. You don't know how much weight you take off me with that promise.

"I figure it out, and now, go to sleep and do it without worries. You have done a good deed and that should help you calmly fall asleep. But above all, try to forget what you have heard, so that this guy cannot suspect you. Realize that you don't know anything and that I am the one who does.

"I will try to follow your advice. You are going to help me and you also deserve a peaceful sleep.

"I plan to sleep with the tranquility of the just, even if I don't have much of it.

"Don't say those things. You are the kindest and most gentleman man who has ever set foot in the West.

"And maybe the craziest and stupid, but… Okay, let's put this down. Come on, you will be surrendered. We will discuss the matter later.

The girl, calmer, left the gambler's home and went to her accommodation. She did it with all modesty, so as not to be seen, for she was afraid that, if at such hours she was seen leaving the gambler's house, the comments made about her visit would not be pious for her.

When the young woman had disappeared, Lamore sat down again on the edge of the bed and lit a new pipe.

Betty's revelation revealed new facets to Grant's unclean activities, and she was looking at the matter from various angles.

The arrogant and bombastic Phelps deserved exemplary punishment for that and he would receive it, but the blow had to be applied in a subtle and subterranean way, in order to prevent him from finding out where the blow came from; for if he suspected that Betty had heard everything that had been said that night in the office, the girl would be in terrible danger.

This fear was what was going to force him to study the case very thoroughly, so as not to commit some imprudence that would have tragic repercussions on the unhappy Betty.

And after thinking about the matter many times, he ended up making a drastic decision.

He would look for Caleb and Corny, discover the plot, and then together they would study the counterattack, which had to be tough and exemplary, because with Grant, those who were going to support him in the assault also had to be punished.

Caleb, Corny, and Tyson ate breakfast in the inn's modest dining room. The night before they had returned from Tombstone where the two adventurers had had a new conversation with the director of the La Esperanza mine. Their efforts were very advanced and they already had almost everything ready to get the money from there.

An erect and slender figure, she stopped before the opening of the dining room window and stood still as if distracted.

Recognizing the gambler, Tyson exclaimed:

"Mr. Lamore.

And impetuous, he got up, going to the window.

"Good morning, Mr. Lamore" he greeted.

" Hello boy! Are you here?

"Yes, sir, I have found two men as kind as you and I am going to work in your company. Would you like to spend a moment?

"Well, I'll stop by not to snub you.

The two cowboys greeted him warmly. Lamore sat down after shaking the seat with his handkerchief and commented:

"I haven't seen them since the night of the ruckus. Are they no longer Grant's clients?

"In reality, we are not clients of anybody in particular. We go where we see fit.

" Already! I understand that after that, tempers could flare up again and ... perhaps it is not wise.

" For whom? He asked dismissively, Caleb.

"Well ... for everyone. You never know what is going to happen.

Tyson dared to interrupt him, asking:

"Tell me, Mr. Lamore ... What happened to the girl?

With Betty? Oh well, nothing serious. I allowed myself to intervene and everything was settled.

"I'm glad. That barbarian mistreated her like a coward and she only wishes one day to be able to remind her in a way that she can never forget. Once underground, it is not possible to remember.

"This is all very generous of you, boy. I have never believed that the women who land here are worth taking risks, but I confess that Betty is an exception. Anyway, why talk more about the matter?

And facing Corny, he indicated:

"I understand that you are looking for some men who do not look like the majority of those who swarm around here ... Am I right?

Corny and Caleb looked at each other in surprise, not knowing what to answer. The question was tricky, but it was violent to answer it with an outburst.

Lamore avoided violence, adding:

"Well, you don't really need to answer me. I just wanted to warn you that you may be wrong about certain elements.

The comment startled them. From those evasive words, they were beginning to understand that Cosimo knew a little more about their movements than they supposed.

"What do you mean by that, Mr. Lamore?

"Very little. I can confess that my sympathies are with the men who try to keep themselves upright and decent. For the rest, although I know few of this class, I do know many others from the opposite field. For example, if I had a decent job on my hands that needed help to develop it, I would distrust men like Donald Sttup and Groyn Brandon and would even think that between the first and the last or vice versa, there could be a third closely related who could be me. harmful, if both as friends who are of Grant, were put in combination with him.

Caleb rose impetuously from his seat, exclaiming:

"Mr. Lamore, what do you know about our jobs and those guys?

"Nothing, guys. I only know that, if you have any of them, they will betray you by putting you in danger and since I am a man I do not want to get involved in matters that do not concern me and I do not want to be called a snitch, I limit myself to giving you a personal impression of those guys , so that you keep it in mind, in case at some point you see yourself committed to them.

"Nothing more than that and now, glad to see you well and wishing you good luck if you need to start a trip soon, I say goodbye to you.

And waving graciously, he left the dining room, puzzling the three adventurers. When they reacted, Corny commented:

"Caleb, this has been a full-blown warning, given to us by that man in a subtle and skillful way. Something knows about our next trip and warns us to be very careful with Brandon.

"Well, why refer to Sttup and Grant? We have not dealt with Sttup, because we know him and less with Grant.

"Yes, but I think that what he has tried to make us understand is that Brandon must have informed Sttup and he must have informed Grant. If so, it can be assumed that, if they try to ambush us, who is to organize it is Grant and who has to direct it is Sttup.

"I'm afraid you are right. They must have formed a chain and we are in serious danger.

"We could have run it, but not anymore. The warning has been providential and I wonder how Lamore found out.

"He works at the gambling den. Perhaps some recklessness of those guys has put him on guard and wanted to warn us. Lamore is a gambler, but an honest gambler.

"We have to clear that up before it's too late. I'm going to get Brandon and ...

"Calm down! We won't do any of that, because it doesn't suit us. Things will develop normally until the critical moment of setting out. So they will believe that we live ignorant of what they are up to and they will trust themselves. At the last minute, we will take drastic measures and you will be in for a surprise as you are not expecting. Let's forget this as if we knew nothing and continue treating Brandon as if we considered him as an angel with rose-colored wings.

"What we are going to do right now is go to Tombstone to talk to the people in charge of the mine and study what can be done to have everything planned.

"Seem right. Let's go for a horse ride. And turning to Tyson, he added:

"You will stay here in case something happens; you don't have a horse and you would be a hindrance. Tonight we will be back.

"Well, I will do what I am ordered to do.

Corny drew a small revolver from his back pocket and examined it. Then he offered it to the boy, saying:

"Here, it is convenient that you carry it in your pocket if you do not want to wear it on your belt. You never know what can happen to you.

"Thanks. I have a little apprehension about weapons, but I understand that here you cannot live detached from them and I will try to get used to their handling.

The two cowboys left the dining room and a quarter of an hour later, they were riding towards the mining center.

Tyson stayed at the inn most of the morning without leaving it. For the first time, he had been alone since he became friends with his two strange companions and he wanted to take advantage of that loneliness to review the accidents of his past adventures and look a bit ahead.

Without realizing it, he was beginning to put a strange and new twist on his existence. He had always been a calm and peaceful man and now, by the whims of fate, he was going to be forced to acclimatize to the harsh environment of the mining basin, joining with more or less success the legion of determined men, who were obliged to debate between danger if they wanted to defend themselves and live. A strange paradox, but one that had to be accepted with all its consequences or deserted cowardly. At heart, he was not a coward, but he was afraid of lacking the conditions and serenity to show it.

A soldier in war needs to get used to hearing fearlessly the thunder of weapons and familiarizing himself with the danger and he had not yet gone through such a trance to assess how far he could go to get in tune with his companions.

Between being forced to become a robber out of hunger and despair, running the same dangers, or exposing his life for a noble cause, he preferred the latter. And if it turned out well, he would earn money and being a sparing man, he could save money for later returning to the East to start a new life. Apparently they paid well for the job, and the benefit was well worth the risk.

After this dispassionate examination of his situation and firmly asserting himself in his decisions, he seemed to feel calmer and more self-assured. He no longer had doubts about the future and would follow his path, bad or good, with a firm and sure step.

In the afternoon, he lay down for a while and, in the evening, went out for a walk in the village.

This one was beginning to perk up. The night owls, satisfied their sleep, took to the street to finish waking up and that seemed an anthill in which human ants were even more dangerous than the red ones of the jungle.

Tyson walked away towards the outskirts. He disliked this environment and seemed to feel little at home among these guys, whose revolvers hung low, almost hit them in the knees and were something that looked more than they.

He was reaching the less populated part to the north, when, descending a narrow and pine street, with a road covered with dust, he discovered a female silhouette advancing in the opposite direction, almost glued to the facades to be inconspicuous.

Tyson, who had already observed the few women who circulated through the streets of the town, especially at the hours when the adventurers took over the roads, believed that it was one of the girls who performed in Grant's joint and the he looked curiously, but suffered a strange shudder, thinking he recognized Betty in her.

He guessed it was her because of her slim figure, her distinguished air, and the severe modesty with which she dressed. Neither her skirt, nor her blouse, nor her air, were anything like the appearance and attire of the others.

And he was glad to find her. Since the night he exposed himself to being shot down for defending her, he had not seen her and it was a pleasure for him to face her again.

And overcoming her indecision, she ran to the opposite side to cut her off.

Betty, realizing this, tried to rectify her path and change to the opposite side, to avoid the encounter, but she too had just recognized the young man and the gratitude for his trait in taking his side, seemed to oblige her not to do such contempt.

And with an effort of will he continued to advance, wondering what the boy's attitude was.

When he got close to her, he gallantly took off his shabby hat and saluted saying:

Good afternoon, Miss Betty.

"Good afternoon sir. Call me dry Betty, because here people use few compliments, especially with us.

"I don't care how others behave but how I should behave. I don't know how I would treat the others, yes.

"Why that distinction?

"Well, because I know that you are not like the others.

"Who could tell you so?

"A person who seems to know you well and who deserves a lot of credit for me.

"There is only one here capable of talking about me like that.

"Then it has to be the same.

"Have you seen her, after… that?

The girl asked the question shyly. Lamore had not given him an account of his efforts to prevent both Caleb and Corny from being surprised by the ambush they were trying to set up and he burned to know something concrete.

"Yes" Tyson affirmed innocently "this morning he was at the inn with my companions and me.

"Ah! "She exclaimed with relief." And did he talk about something interesting for you?

"A lot, Miss Betty.

"You don't know what makes me happy and reassures me that Lamore has warned them of the danger they may be in.

Tyson was on guard when he heard her. Instinct told him that she was also in on the secret of what was threatening them, and he decided to get some more details from the girl about the vagrants that the gambler had indicated.

"Yes" he affirmed, "he told us everything.

"I'm glad. I already knew that he would do something. I confess I was terribly frightened when I caught Sttup's conversation with Grant and heard them planning the wagon robbery so cowardly. I could do nothing, but he could, and that same night I went to his accommodation and told him about everything.

Tyson bit his lip, not daring to comment on the situation. He had forced the girl to discover herself betraying without bad faith the discretion of the gambler, who had not wanted to bring Betty to the fore.

Regretful of his unconscious behavior, he begged:

"Listen, Miss Betty, I beg you not to talk about this meeting and what we have talked about, telling Lamore about it.

"Why if he ...?

"Excuse me. He warned us to be careful with Brandon and Sttup and Grant on the mission we apparently had on our hands, but he neither said nor alluded to you at all. His discretion and his desire to leave you out of the matter forced him to act with great discretion and he did not give us any details of what was being plotted against us, he did not even allude to how he had known. Perhaps she would be angry if she knew that I had forced her to reveal herself, although I swear as far as one can swear, that not even a word that could harm her would be shot out of my body.

The girl was confused for a moment, but then, with resolution, she looked him face to face, saying:

"I believe you and I have no objection to affirming that I heard everything and I can give you all the details I captured. My conscience forces me to speak, and even if it brought me grave danger, it would not keep my secret.

"You are admirable, Betty, and I don't know how to praise you without taking my words gallantly. If, as you say, you don't mind telling us everything, I would appreciate it if you could give me some more detail that could be of great use to us.

"I have no problem. I will say nothing to Lamore nor to you either, but it is convenient that they know everything exactly.

And as they walked toward the center of town, he gave her a brief but concise account of the conversation that had surprised those two rascals.

He listened to her in silence and walked beside her. As he crossed one of the cross streets to the main one, Tyson looked distractedly at the other side, and at the door of a tavern, chatting with a stranger, he discovered Brandon, with whom he had already dealt with his companions. The traitor saw him perfectly accompanying Betty and Tyson also noticed Brandon, but did not give any importance to the meeting. This was a mistake she would later regret and Betty too.

The young woman ended her story and Tyson stiffly replied:

"You don't know how much I appreciate the details that are going to be of great use to us. No wonder Mr. Lamore really appreciates you and I join him. It's a shame she's forced to act under pressure from that poisonous toad.

"It is, but I have no choice.

Why don't you try to get out of their clutches?

"I wish I could, but it's not possible at least for now. Anyway, let's not talk about that which has no immediate remedy.

" Who knows! You have inspired me with great confidence and great affection and you are so interesting to me that who knows if we can still break your chains. Not by myself, who am insignificant, but helped by my friends who are tough and very good men. They also have to thank her for the warning that she is going to save us all from being cowardly murdered and I know that they are men who do not forget the good or the bad.

"Very grateful for your interest, but better leave it that way for now. Someday ... Anyway, I beg you to leave me. We'll head over to the Tombstone Bar and if Grant saw me in his company we might all be sorry.

"It's easy even him. I do not know why my heart tells me that one day we will face each other again to pay off the debt that night, but this time it will not be in inferior conditions on my part; now I know what kind of reptile it is and it wouldn't take me by surprise.

"You better never have to face him and I would be sorry it was because of me. He is too harsh an enemy for your teeth and I am not saying this in an attempt to offend you.

"I am not offended because I know how far I can go, but I have plenty of heart to make up for my lack of practice and I fight for justice and good.

"Not in front of a revolver handled with little nobility.

She stopped, willing not to continue the dialogue or to allow him to continue accompanying her. Tyson followed suit and, holding out his hand, asked:

" Friends from the heart?

She handed him hers, saying excitedly:

"Thanks.

And quickly, she started walking towards the joint.

Tyson veered toward the inn. The Night was spreading its dark cloak and I was apprehensive of wandering at such hours.

His companions would soon be back from Tombstone, and he wanted to tell them about his encounter with Betty and all that she had revealed to him.

He understood that while they should thank Lamore for the valuable advice he had given them, the greatest thanks were due to this brave and unfortunate girl, who was the one who had exposed the cowardly ambush that Grant and his satellites were rigging against them.

While he was waiting impatiently for the arrival of the two cowboys, at the joint, Sttup was interviewing Grant to say:

"I spoke with Brandon for a moment and he told me that tomorrow he will know when everything is organized for the game and the itinerary to follow.

"Very well. Nothing more?

" Oh yeah! He has told me something that interests you.

" What is it about?

"Brandon just told me that when he was at the door of Walter's tavern, he saw Betty go by with that guy, because of whose cause you armed the fat woman the other night. They seemed very animated and I am letting you know so that you are aware.

Grant gritted his teeth, saying:

"Thanks for the news. I'm not very concerned about the guy because, as you know, his hours are numbered, but when this is resolved, I swear to you that a lot of things will happen. I'm sick of this flirt making fun of me and I am a man who when he loses his patience, does not repair solutions, whatever they are. It does not matter because, surely, he must have sought her out to ingratiate himself with her for her gesture that night; but even so I do not admit that nobody crosses my path, that I want it smooth and clear. My plans about that stupid rebel are outlined and there will be no one who crosses my path, if they do not want to go and raise mallows in the cemetery.

"It's okay, Grant. I have fulfilled a duty notifying you, the rest is up to you.

"And I appreciate it, but that can wait a couple of days or three. What interests me is the other. Only when Brandon gives us complete details regarding the expedition, will I be happy because I will arrange everything in detail so that this coveted silver comes to our hands.

It was quite late when the two adventurers returned from Tombstone. They returned tired but satisfied with what had been discussed with the leaders of the mine. Tyson, with a strange gleam in his eyes, exclaimed:

"I was eager to see you again.

"Is something wrong? Caleb asked suspiciously.

"Many things happen that interest us all. I know the whole plan outlined to send us to hell and be able to seize the wagon with the silver.

"What do you say, boy? Caleb exclaimed. You're not going to tell me that you went to ask Grant, or that you forced Brandon to speak out of time.

"Nothing of that. I haven't seen any, but I have talked to the person who heard it all and then told Lamore. It was Betty.

" What are you saying?

"Yes, she heard it from her dressing room and rushed to find Cosimo to try something to avoid it. Lamore did not dare to be more explicit, fearing compromising the girl and withheld details from us that were too precious to us to have the whole plot in hand. Listen.

And he gave them an account of everything he had discussed with Betty. The two surprised cowboys heard the details and Tyson excitedly exclaimed:

"They won't tell me that girl is not worth a treasure!

"Right, Tyson, maybe… he did everything in gratitude to you for your gallant intervention on his behalf. It seems to me good that you speak with such enthusiasm of her and until ... you interest yourself more than necessary.

Tyson blushed at the insinuation.

"No, I ... Well, well ..., I appreciate her because I know she is good and we are even going to owe her our lives.

"You don't know Tyson women. If you like it, don't lose hope because you listen well; A diamond can fall into the mud, but it will always be a diamond for the one who discovers it and takes it out of the mire. And now we're going to dinner and then we're going to find Brandon. I'm going to give you instructions for tomorrow so that you have time to brief Grant and his satellite.

Almost midnight they left the inn to go to Walter's tavern, where they were to find the traitor. There he was waiting and when he saw them he asked with badly disguised anxiety:

"Everything settled, Caleb?

"Everything, Brandon. Tomorrow at ten o'clock at night you will wait for us in Tombstone, in the City Bar and there we will pick you up to start the march.

"What time will we leave?

"About three in the morning.

"Are we going to Tucson? Well, I don't care much where, but I would like to know if we go there, because at the same time I would solve an issue that interests me in the town.

"Well, don't worry, you can solve it, because we are going there, by the shortest way.

"I'm glad. I suppose you have taken all the measures to be safe. You already know this.

"Yes. We will go six in total and there will be quite a few. Tyson will drive the wagon and we will guard it.

"Not bad. At least the five of us will be worth a dozen.

"This is how we hope that it will happen, as well as we hope that everything will go well despite the risk. We have kept it very secret and we are all involved, trustworthy people.

"Not doubt about it.

The trio, with a somber air, left the tavern to go in search of the other two elements that were to accompany them. Of these, Corny was sure because he knew them very well.

* * *

The next night in Tombstone, Brandon was waiting impatiently for the cowboys. Everything had been well planned to attack them on the trail when they rolled away from the mining field, in a place that lent itself to ambush.

At ten, Caleb and Corny showed up at the City Bar to pick up the traitor.

"Come on, Brandon" said the first one, "they are waiting for us at the mine and everything is ready.

The three of them went out. Outside, Tyson was waiting.

They headed for the mines. Next to Esperanza a barracks was erected where the other two involved in the company waited, as well as the chief engineer and the senior manager.

Next to the barracks two carts, apparently loaded with straw, were waiting.

Brandon glanced at them and was intrigued. It was my understanding that the shipment was reduced to a single cart, and if there were two, the loot was going to be fantastic.

Unable to hide his curiosity, he asked:

"Are we going to take both? I thought it was just one.

"Both will go, but don't worry, everything will be fine.

They entered the pavilion. Without knowing why, he felt uneasy, for it seemed to him that the faces of those gathered there were tense and gloomy.

Caleb, with perfect calm, said:

"Well, we are going to distribute the work.

Made a gesture. Corny, who had come to stand next to Brandon, with a quick, forceful movement seized the traitor's holster and ripped it from his holstered gun belt.

Brandon jumped white and stammered:

"What… what… does this mean?

"Nothing, don't be alarmed; so we can do things more safely.

And coming closer to him and pointing his revolver at him, he said coldly:

"Well, boy, now you are going to tell us everything you have plotted to seize the silver and eliminate us all.

The traitor felt himself caught by the sharp teeth of a trap and trembling with panic, he cried out:

" They are crazy? I am a loyal man and ...

"Agree. Loyal, but to whom? And since we are not here to waste time, I will tell you one thing. We know your confidences with Sttup, the plans he and Grant have hatched to attack us en route, and the job you've been assigned. You will speak?

" That's a lie! Me...

Caleb flicked his arm and punched him fiercely in the mouth. The bandit, spitting some teeth in the blood, bellowed:

"It's false, false ...! I have nothing to confess ...

This time it was Corny who beat him ruthlessly. The undesirable rolled on the floor of the barracks writhing in pain, while the witnesses of the dramatic scene watched him impassively.

Brandon still did not want to confess and the two friends, furious, began to beat and kick with him. The beating was so devastating that Brandon, unable to bear it any longer, cried out wildly:

"Enough! Enough! I'll talk!

"Start soon! Caleb exclaimed without allowing her to get up off the ground.

"Sttup ordered it to me when he found out I was in business with you. He threatened to kill me if I didn't find out about his plans and I had to. They have ambushed nine men on the path, behind some slopes that there are, before reaching a village called Land and there they will attack them by surprise.

"And what is your role in this beautiful game?

"I ... well ... had to support them as much as I could.

"You had to assassinate Tyson in the first place, for being the least dangerous, and immediately shoot down those closest to you, depending on the assault.

" Nerd; not that! ... I just ...

"Enough! I know the plan down to the smallest detail and I will not be fooled by anyone, nor will I have any mercy on treacherous assassins like you. Corny will give it to you.

Brandon, guessing what awaited him, lunged at Corny desperately as he pulled the revolver.

In the short fight, when the bandit tried to snatch the gun from the cowboy, what he did was force him to squeeze the hammer and the bullet hit his throat and Brandon fell to the ground as if struck down.

Tyson covered his eyes, unable to resist the scene, but his companions coldly prepared to act.

"Go ahead" Caleb ordered. This is not going to interrupt our plans or prevent the shipment from reaching its destination. We are going to prepare the stage apparatus.

Between the two friends they took Brandon's body and carried him out. It took them a quarter of an hour to return.

"All set" Caleb said "us to our wagon.

The two chariots with the hitched horses were ready. Caleb ordered one of the two assistants he had:

"You already know what to do, don't you? You know the path and the place where they planned to attack us.

"Don't worry, everything will be done as you have arranged.

"As soon as you're done, come back and stay at the mine until we go. If you showed up alone in the village, you might be suspected and you would be in danger. Walk away!

The others got into the wagon loaded with the silver and Tyson, overcoming the nervousness that seized him, took over the driving. The vehicle followed the route marked by Caleb.

Tyson nervously dared to ask:

"If they wait for us on the path, what will happen?

"Nothing, because they won't get to see us in it. We are going to roll down a less easy but safer road and far from where they have ambushed us. We will go back to the path, but much higher.

* * *

Donald Sttup, with eight well-armed men, had ambushed some slopes that boxed in the trail a few miles from Fairbank and farther, though not much from Tombstone.

According to his calculations, at dawn, the cart loaded with silver had to roll close to the slopes and although the time could be dangerous in case early risers were circulating on the road, it was not in his power to choose the place and time of the assault.

Meanwhile, the cart that was to serve as a claim, rolled slowly and in its box something diabolical had been devised that was going to cause anger and surprise to the assailants.

The man Caleb singled out for her, carrying a shapeless bundle at her side, covered by burlap and securely attached to the box.

It was Brandon's body, but no one could suspect that it was because of the camouflage.

The driver, perfectly calm, did the whole day driving the cart, but when he approached the place of the trap, he descended, stripped the dead man of his cover, leaving him in the box as if he were really the driver and after prodding the tired horses so that continued his journey, he hastened to disappear to undertake the return to Tombstone.

The weary animals, guided by their own instincts, continued to advance without deviating from the route

Dawn was about to break when Sttup, who was keeping watch on the crest of one of the slopes, discovered the cart moving slowly. From his observatory he could perfectly recognize the straw seines that crowned the load.

" Attention! He ordered, smiling wryly. Prepare the rifles, don't fire until I order it because Brandon is among them.

Crouching like rabbits, they followed the progress of the cart with bright eyes. There was a large loot that would provide them with a good handful of dollars to satisfy their vices.

The vehicle was already close when Sttup got up, looking closely.

"Rays of hell! "He murmured." I would swear by the silhouette that the one driving the wagon is Brandon. Why?

"Maybe" said one, dismissive "because that rookie was afraid and had no courage to drive.

"You may be right, but I don't like that at all.

He kept waiting with his nerves tense as the vehicle moved forward and his unease increased in degree when he observed something unusual.

"Blood of Satan! He bellowed. What happens to Brandon who wobbles like he's sleepwalking?

And guessing that something unexpected had happened, he bellowed:

"Down with everyone and imitate me in what I do!

The first leaped like a deer and set foot on the trail, crying out:

"Stop or we'll riddle you with bullets! We are a lot.

No one answered and the wagon moved slowly forward. Sttup advanced, putting himself in front of the animals. They stopped and it was then that he understood the whole truth.

Brandon, with his face contorted by the grimace of death and also accusing of the marks of the punches he received, showed his shirt stained with blood and the ligatures that held him to the box.

Everyone was tense at the discovery. They had mocked them and, in addition, they had killed the most useful of their auxiliaries.

Sttup, madly, ordered the wagon to be searched, but it only carried the corpse and straw seines.

When the bandit climbed onto the box, hurling curses, he saw a piece of paper on the neckline of the dead man's vest. He tugged at it in anger and upon examining it, it emitted an impressive roar.

He had written a few words of bloody derision that said:

«For Grant, Sttup and other angels of the

Averno, with all our respects,

"Caleb and Corny"

The bandits were puzzled. They could not guess how that pair of tough cowboys had been able to discover the plot carried with so much secrecy and how they had been able to evade the ambush.

Sttup was afraid to return to Fairbank to tell Grant of the terrible failure. He knew of his power and his means of elimination and he feared his wrath. Before returning unsuccessful, they had to try something.

And haranguing his men, he roared:

"Guys, this doesn't mean it all. I don't know how they found out about our plans and were able to fool them, but they still haven't succeeded. The silver has to be transferred to Tucson and it has surely followed a different path, while they put this bait ahead of us. You have to find them quickly, even if you have to search the entire basin.

"Where the hell do you think we're going to find them? "One of the gang grumbled." Namely, if they've repented and put it off for another day, or they're shooting so well protected that all we'd get is to get us stupidly killed. That attempt is very dangerous.

"Would you rather face Grant saying that you have failed?

" Why not? The loser will be him. We didn't know what to do until you brought us here and told us what it was about, so the secret was between you and him. If either of the two has been a loudmouth who trumpeted it so that it would reach the ears of those guys, there you guys.

Sttup was thoughtful. The bandit was right and since he hadn't opened his mouth at all and even his men were ignorant of what it was about if there was any indiscretion it must have been Grant's fault. Let him bear the consequences and discover the snitch who betrayed them.

And since apparently his men weren't willing to take a risk without making sure of the chances of success beforehand, he had no choice but to resign himself and head to the village.

When he got to Fairbank late at night, he headed for the joint.

Grant still worried about what might be happening on the trail, he did not expect to have news until the next day, so it was a surprise for him to see Sttup appear.

With a gesture he motioned for her to come into the office, and soon after she joined him.

Betty, who had seen the gunman enter, felt her blood run cold in her veins. He guessed that he was giving an account of his mission again, but he could not guess what news he was carrying, although from the tenseness of his features he thought he understood that nothing he was going to communicate to Grant would be pleasant to him.

She was tempted to run to the little dressing room in case she could catch the dialogue from there, but a terrible fear invaded her. Once, luck had favored him, but he had to be careful what he did, because if she was surprised by someone and Grant suspected that the one who had taken the plot of prey from him was her, she was capable of killing her coldly.

He would hold his nerves and wait. More or less later he would come to know the truth.

Grant, haunted by a strange foreboding, asked longingly:

"How soon here, Sttup? What happened?

"That's what I have to ask you! What happened for the devil to take everything?

"I do not understand. Do you want to explain?

"Of course I will explain myself. Those pigs knew about everything and they shot Brandon to the throat. Then, they have tied him to the box of a cart loaded only with straw and have thrown it onto the path. When we went out to arrest her, we discovered the body in the box and it was tucked between Brandon's shirt and vest. Here, read:

Grant, green with anger, read the letter. The wildest anger took hold of him.

"Who was the scoundrel who gave the tip?

"That's what I have come to ask you. None of my men knew where they were going or what they had to do. They found out when they were waiting in ambush and since I have only spoken to you about this matter, I am the one who asks you how they were able to discover it.

"Oh, this is to go crazy! "Bellowed Grant." I have not spoken to absolutely anyone other than you. I do not understand how they have been able to discover it.

"Well that happens to me. The point is, we've lost the best loot of our lives.

"Because you are an idiot. You should have assumed that the silver would be taken to Tucson and you should have inquired where.

"It was already my idea, but my men refused. They feared, and perhaps rightly so, that once the plan was discovered, the wagon would be protected in such a way that daring to attack it would be as much as committing suicide.

Grant was puzzled. Chewing the words as he spoke, he growled:

"Oh! We have lost something fabulous and I will not forgive those two guys for their meddling and the failure they have provided us.

"On the other hand, this writing reveals Sttup to me, and you have to cover those mouths with lead so that they cannot speak.

"Since you have not served to seize the loot, at least I hope that you will serve to eliminate them before it is too late. Do not forget that, if they have managed to find out even the smallest detail of the plan, they will not be willing to forgive that we have wanted to send them to hell. Now it is a matter of life or death for them and for us and the smartest and fastest will be the one who wins the game.

And proceed with all your senses, for you are like me sentenced to death. You see that they know your participation in the coup. "

"Okay, but there is something else missing that is up to you to clarify.

" The fact that?

"Someone has had news of our plans and has given the tip. Find that person and shoot them.

"If I knew who he is, he wouldn't live any longer than the time it takes me to find him.

And Sttup left the office as gloomy as he left the ambitious Grant.

As they set out on the journey, contrary to what Caleb and Corny feared, no one tried to locate them on their new route or search for them in Tucson when they happily arrived and delivered the cargo. Everything had been developed too simply and they did not like this, because it did not seem to fit the methods and character of Phelps.

They returned to Tombstone by the same path that they had taken when leaving it and with the same cart. Of the other and the oxen, as well as Brandon's corpse, they did not know a word.

But in the mining town Val Spring was waiting for them, the man who had been assigned with the order to drive the wagon to the vicinity of the ambush site. Spring had gone to the trouble of venturing down the trail the next day. The wagon had moved away to a meadow off the track, where the animals, tired of walking and of their own free will, had stopped, becoming hooked to the vehicle.

There was Brandon's body still tied to the box, but the paper Caleb had slipped into his chest was gone. This indicated that Stupp's crew had discovered the trap.

Spring unhitched the oxen and, leaving the trail, returned with them to Tombstone. The cart and the dead man were left where he found them.

"As she was old and of little value, I didn't want to venture to shoot with her," he said;

"You did good. Everything went wonderfully. What happens next is what to keep in mind.

"What do you mean?

"To whatever Grant has prepared for us to receive us triumphantly.

"We can stay here in Tombstone," he replied.

"We can, but we will not stay for various reasons. One, because it would be as much as showing a fear that we do not feel and the other, because the fact that we have aborted the plan does not erase the intention to cowardly murder ourselves. Both Stupp and Grant have to pay for this ambush and one day I told that gambling toad that I am a guy that when I set out to remember someone I always keep him in my prayers. I think the time has come to pray for the soul of that cowardly pig.

"You have spoken like a book," said Corny. I'm very curious to reach into Grant's stomach to see what kind of scorpions he has inside, and I suspect no occasion like this.

Tyson, who had caught the optimism and courage of his cold companions, intervened to say:

"I also have something to avenge on him. The first bullet was aimed at my back and I would like to return it to him, but in cash.

"That's right, boy, but you'll have to delegate to one of us, because Grant is too much of a gunman for you. You are very green with the colt in hand and we do not want to carry the responsibility of allowing you to commit suicide without any use.

"I will continue to rehearse with the weapon and ...

"And they'll give you the pass when you've served as a leading figure at a funeral. No, boy; just make sure it is someone else who will dispatch him and later you will have the opportunity to rehearse your shooting skills. This is not a joke and we cannot even assume that we will send you to hell easily.

Tyson had to resign himself and agreed to rest one day in the village. They had to collect their stipends, quite large, and had agreed to renew their deteriorated attire that they badly needed.

Caleb commented to the boy:

"When you go to the store, take care of what you choose because don't forget that there, in Fairbank, there is a very interesting girl who has only known you as a beggar and needs to gauge what kind of man you turn out to be dressed as a farmer.

Tyson blushed and said nothing. He had been worrying more than Betty for a few days and no longer dared to deny that he had been more interested than he thought.

And suggested by the recommendation, he was very demanding with the outfit, until he managed to choose a magnificent suede trousers that fit him admirably, a plaid shirt that was the latest in color, a pair of high-heeled and fine half boots that They made him look taller, an elegant stanton hat and a blue neckerchief that looked like a patch of sky on another patch of nearly black, sun-tanned fur.

Afterwards, clean-shaven, his hair trimmed and lustrous with cosmetics and scents, he looked like someone else. So much so that Corny exclaimed:

"Well, boy, if as soon as you arrive and see you, she doesn't open her arms and fall into yours asking you to take her to the pastor, I lose my earnings from the trip.

"Don't scoff," Tyson stammered "; That girl hasn't noticed me at all and I'm ... I'm too small for her.

"Now do you think so? Come on, don't be a pumpkin. Nobody is more than anyone when you manage to interest another person. Betty deserves a good boy and you are. Someday you will find a good and secure job, or you will save enough and you can take her out of here like a gentleman. The girl only needs that to leave this hell happier than a few Easter.

Since they all owned a horse except Tyson, it was agreed to help him acquire one and they all gave a few dollars on their behalf to purchase the mount. She couldn't be out of tune with her, apart from the fact that at any moment she might be very much needed.

And already well equipped and with money in their pockets, they decided to return to Fairbank.

But as they walked into the village, Caleb noticed:

"And now, watch out. We will not commit the foolishness of entering there by the path in a straight line, since it is certain that they are waiting for our arrival to celebrate it with hardware salvos. It will not be very impressive, but it will be more secure. Later ... we'll talk.

The cowboy's prudent measure was highly justified, for from the very day that Stupp returned unsuccessfully, one of the first measures he had taken was to ambush four men on the outskirts of Fairbank with the order to rigorously guard the trail and take in You shoot the return of your enemies.

Stupp used to go two or three times a day to the place where he had left his men watching, a half-ruined and abandoned house on the edge of the trail, and after those visits, to maintain the discipline of his henchmen and to encourage them not to be careless in the field. vigilance, sure that they would return sooner or later, he returned to the village where he was devoting himself to his usual life.

Sometimes he spent some time in the "Tombstone Bar," but very little, to avoid being suspected of his intimacy with Grant, and sometimes he spent a few hours in Walter's tavern, drinking or playing poker with some fellow gamblers.

Grant, for his part, had also taken precautions and had around him four gunmen ready to defend him if he was attacked by someone.

Caleb, Corny and their three companions entered Fairbank without incident or being discovered thanks to the precautions taken. They did it from the west instead of entering from the east, as it seemed necessary, and therefore no one noticed their arrival

They went directly to the inn and then held a kind of court martial to match their conduct to the circumstances.

Corny hinted:

"My opinion is that we must take the initiative immediately. I am sure that they are waiting for us to claim failure and before they have time to prepare, we are the ones who must fight. If we can take someone by surprise, we will have won.

"Sounds good to me," said Caleb, "but they may have turned the joint into a fortress and it's not as easy to get into as you think.

"We will test the waters wisely.

And with determination they took to the street distanced from each other to offer less target and searching with their eyes along the street in case danger arose unexpectedly before them.

But apparently no one had noticed their presence in the village and this favored them for the moment.

As they crossed in front of Walter's tavern, Caleb had a hunch and, gesturing for his friends to stop, crossed the dark driveway and stepped into the doorway of the tavern to take a discreet look inside.

And a wry smile folded his hard lips as he discovered Stupp inside, playing poker with two of his most trusted men.

There was one of the two most directly responsible for the unsuccessful ambush. As it seemed as if the bill began to be passed on for him as for Grant, the cowboy stepped back to join the others.

"Get ready, Corny," he warned. The hunt is about to begin.

"What's going on? Corny asked.

"That there is Stupp playing with two of his best buddies. As can be logically assumed that all three have taken part in the affair, we are going to start handing out cash prizes.

"Agree. Lead is a metal, although quite poor and those do not deserve a better one.

The group moved forward, but Caleb energetically said:

"Careful; nothing to assault the establishment en masse as if we were going to fight with an army; For those three guys it's quite a lot Corny and me. You will be left out in case we need you.

"But" Tyson intervened "this matter belongs to everyone and we must ...

"Children to shut up," Caleb replied. When you grow up and your time comes you will eat soups. Come on, man, go ahead.

The two cowboys stepped forward and their companions stood by the doorway, not daring to contravene the rough Caleb's orders. He was the first to push the rotating blade past, though Corny stuck to him to keep up.

Stupp had been distracted and was playing almost with his back to the door. He did not even remotely suspect being surprised by his enemies and this caused him to fall into the surprise that he had tried so hard to avoid.

The two cowboys took several steps forward and before reaching the table, Caleb yelled cheerfully:

"Devil, but our dear friend Stupp is here.

The latter, as if he had been bitten by a viper, dropped the cards and jumped to his feet, being imitated by his two companions. The three of them, telepathically in agreement, reached for the colts and pulled them desperately.

The maneuver was too slow despite how quickly they tried to put into aggressive action. By the time their weapons fired inaccurately, the two cowboys' two revolvers had already thundered four times with deadly aim, and the booms of their opponent's weapons echoed theirs. The projectiles went misdirected without hitting the audacious couple.

There were still new shots from her to make sure they did not have the courage to defend themselves and when the three in a confused and bloody heap fell to the ground dragging tables and benches in their spectacular fall, the two cowboys, blowing the cannons of their colts to fan the faint column of smoke that seemed to still come out of the interior, they calmly holstered, while Caleb commented:

"Well, Stupp, this matter is settled. I'm afraid you won't have the courage to organize more surprises as cowardly as you were.

And pushing his partner out, he forced him to leave the establishment with him, astonishing customers who had barely had time to follow the drama in its swift bloody phases.

"Issue resolved," said Caleb, pushing out the rest of his friends who were impetuously trying to enter as soon as they had caught the shots. The matter was resolved with an ease that I am ashamed of. We are going to make a similar visit to the "Tombstone Bar" to see if we solve this matter completely and with the same luck.

But Grant, more shrewd and suspicious, was not a man to be easily surprised. From the moment he learned of the ambush's failure, he took all sorts of precautions. Not only had he installed four members of the gang on the premises to protect him, but he barely showed himself in the gambling den. He was waiting for his enemies to show up in some way so he would know how to proceed.

His five enemies, hands resting on the hilt of the revolver for good measure, came in a group into the joint and eagerly searched for Grant, but Grant was not visible.

Instead, they discovered certain faces that Caleb and Corny were very familiar with as Stupp's friends. It did not take a lynx to guess that their presence there obeyed the slogan of ensuring the life of the presumed owner of the premises.

The first, with a strange movement, made the colt appear in his hand, juggling with it by spinning it on his finger tucked next to the percussion, while saluting:

"Good evening, gentlemen. Hello, you and Sam, Andersen. I find you here too calm when down there in Walter's tavern you were missing more than here. I have heard that your great friend Stupp has suffered a fatal accident, as well as two of his companions and perhaps you are more interested in praying something to him so that he will not be rejected in hell when he arrives.

The four stiffened, but faithful to the slogan they had received, one of them replied:

"Caleb, don't you think you've been living on tip for some time?

"It is possible, boy, but here we all live on tips, some more and others less, like Stupp, for example. Don't you think you are too much?

"Possibly, but I don't like loneliness and the day I start the great trip I plan to be in good company.

"That's fine, boy, but if you don't want to hit the road tonight, the best you can do is forget that you wear those toys around your waist. It is an advice that I give you, although I will not charge you anything for giving it to you.

"We do not think to use it if someone does not insist on showing us the eye of theirs. -

"A wise decision. What does our elegant friend Grant think of that? I'd like to hear your opinion.

Grant is in Tombstone. He had business to resolve there and he left.

"What a pity! Didn't he pass out up there and you haven't realized it? I would like to check it out personally.

He intended to move into the gambling den, but one of the gunmen who had taken up residence by the door phlegmatically warned:

"If I were in their shoes, I would settle for what they have told them.

"Why?

"Not for nothing, I suspect it's very dark and you might trip and hurt yourself entering.

Caleb caught the threatening meaning of the warning. He would be shot and all the advantage would be on the side of his opponent.

"I will have to believe that it is true that he was absent. Do you know if it will take a long time to return?

"He didn't say anything about his return.

"Well, we can wait a bit because we are not in a hurry. With such pleasant company, one is as good here as sitting on a powder keg with the fuse lit, and that always has its charm. Give us something to drink.

They sat strategically at a table attached to the wall from which they dominated the entire premises and the entrance door to the interior. Caleb put the colt on the tabletop and his teammates followed suit. It was like a terrible battery ready to sweep the premises at the slightest attempt at aggression.

A great nervousness seized most of the customers despite the fact that they were men familiar with that environment and its dangers. Everyone guessed that any misinterpreted move would trigger a battle that could be tragic.

But no one dared to show that they were afraid and although with all their senses alert, they prepared to continue drinking and playing.

The four gunmen, puzzled, did not know what to do. They had five well-disposed enemies in front of them, and it was foolhardy to take initiatives.

If Grant chose not to show himself, the matter might end up in a stalemate and no one would decide to be the first to pull the trigger.

Caleb ordered a bottle of whiskey and then yelled:

"What happens that this looks like a funeral? Master, let music come to cheer the hearts of these people a little.

The teacher hastened to sit down at the piano. The music played sourly, but no one seemed up to dancing.

Lamore, sitting on his high stool, had followed the scene with interest. The game had been paralyzed in the first moments and he was able to fix his attention on that tough quintet that did not know fear and had not hesitated to seek the enemy in their own den.

As for Betty, she seemed fascinated by everything that was happening. She was glancing at the five of them and her attention seemed more focused on Tyson, whom she had almost unknown. Now, seeing him dressed again, clean and neat, he seemed a good-looking man as he had not supposed through his deteriorated garb.

Caleb, who was calling the shots, said:

"Tyson, I think you should dance with Betty for a bit. He is the best partner you can find and I do not think that now no one dares to stop you from doing it. Come on, boy, go ahead and let these friends see what good dancers you are.

Tyson, who was waking up next to that couple of strange and tough guys, did not make himself beg and going ahead, without waiting for her to agree or refuse, he linked her by the waist and took her out on the track.

The young woman, tense and apparently cold to give the impression that she was agreeing under pressure and threat, allowed herself to be carried away, but in a low voice, she pleaded:

Please tell me what happened!

"Nothing. Brandon died as a traitor and we carry the money elsewhere. All without news.

"Grant is biting. He's scared and he's hiding in there, but don't say it because he's armed to the teeth and he's accompanied by two gunmen.

"Thanks. Stupp has also disappeared. My friends have just given it what it deserved.

"And now that?

"I do not know. They want to undo the band, but I'm afraid it will take work. I'd like to see you.

"It's not possible. Beware, because it would hurt me. Grant rages at Knowing who could discover the plan and constantly threatens to kill anyone if he discovers it.

"Leave him.

"It is not possible now, because I have nowhere to go. I'll have to wait and see what happens.

"I will help her as soon as I can.

He had finished the piece. Tyson released the young woman, saying:

"Thanks; You dance very well, but you are unsympathetic because of how not very talkative it is. When I learn to speak how she dances I will take her out again.

She, with a contemptuous gesture, turned her back on him.

The five friends in the joint continued drinking and sowing nervousness in the attendees. This seemed to amuse them, because they showed no signs of wanting to leave the premises.

Late at night, Caleb got up saying:

"Well, it seems Grant is delaying his return. What if we left?

"We'll be back tomorrow to see if we have more luck," Corny said seriously.

"Then lets go.

Caleb stayed where he was as his teammates headed for the exit. The tough cowboy protected his march from the possibility of an attack from behind.

When they reached the doorway, they stopped, showing their faces. Caleb joined them and the four of them went forward so as not to lose any movement of their opponents.

"Bye, guys" said Caleb "; Don't bother going out to say goodbye because there's a deadly air blowing out there. You could catch a lead cold.

He disappeared. No one dared to move, for they knew what the warning meant. They could be in front of the door waiting for someone to show up to shoot him down.

But the tension was gone. No one had won a single trick in the game and it was left in the air for a more propitious occasion.

The three friends, before retiring to rest that night, exchanged views on the latest events and were content to appreciate that, although they had taught Grant a good lesson and deprived him of some of his best elements, the game was not won. and that from then on they would have to walk with leaden feet, since it would be very difficult and exposed to try to get rid of the dirty adventurer and he could instead plot new plots against them.

Furthermore, it was debated whether or not it was convenient to move to Tombstone for a while, but Tyson was against it, because he understood that after the immense service that Betty had rendered them, it was cowardly to leave her abandoned. Tyson feared that whatever circumstance Grant suspected that she was the one who thwarted his plans by giving the blow, and he was afraid of what might happen to the young woman if this happened.

Caleb commented:

"You are taking a great interest in the girl, Tyson.

"Perhaps, but I am only corresponding to his behavior. Not to mention the rest.

"Okay, boy; I think you are right, apart from the fact that if we disappeared, they would suspect that we had been scared off and this would embolden them. After all, if they want to try something against us, they can do the same thing here as in Tombstone. Here you can take advantage of a favorable moment to pass the bill to Phelps, while down there ... Anyway, we will stay, but for now I have to go back to Tombstone. I have left pending to finalize a very good matter that, if it comes together, will assure us work and income for a good season.

"More silver pipes? Tyson asked anxiously.

"Yes and no, little one, but something that will make you happy if it is done. The manager of "Esperanza" suggested to me the idea of forming a body of mine guards to protect and transfer the silver to the banks where it is destined and to set up a service where it is needed. They want us to organize it on behalf of the most prominent miners in the basin who do not know themselves safe among this legion of undesirables and are willing to pay very well. We will have a secure job, good income and lead to chew more than once, but ... the bad thing is that for that we need men who do not look like most of those who are here and that is not easy to find. If we can solve it, our concerns will be over for some time and whoever knows how to take advantage of the streak, if he does not take down an ounce of lead,

"Oh, it would be wonderful if it did, Caleb! Tyson enthusiastically replied. I would be one of those who saved every penny for later ...

"Yes," Corny interrupted smiling, "kidnap Betty, take her east, found a banking house and make her the queen of finance.

"Oh, not so much! I think Betty is not ambitious and with being free from this environment and from Grant's clutches, she will feel very happy. She and I would settle for a quiet little farm at the foot of a mountain in a quiet green valley where ...

"Stop it, boy, don't get too excited," Caleb cried out. Have you asked Betty if that is her taste and if you are hers?

"Well, no, but... I'm sure I'm not wrong.

"You're an optimist, Tyson, and that's good, but just in case, you better take advantage of your time with Corny instead of thinking about it so prematurely and take a few revolver lessons. If things work out, you will have to be one of many and not live under daddy's skirts to protect you. Carefully rehearse that the lives of men here are enclosed in an ounce of lead inside the barrel of a colt.

The following day, Caleb mounted a horse and left for Tombstone, while Corny and Tyson, also on horseback, headed to the outskirts of the town, where the second had to carry out severe practices under the experience of the cowboy, who would be in charge of the training of the young man. .

The aggressive visit of the three adventurers made the night before to Grant's joint, confirmed to him in his suspicions that his life would not be worth a berry, as long as those tough and risky guys remained on their feet with the intention of wielding a revolver and, as his life "for him" was worth more than that of a hundred enemies put together, he had to do something to guarantee it.

Too many worries, he already possessed, and too many dangers he had left behind to create new ones. Grant was one of those who was never trusted, because his activities had always been so doubtful and unscrupulous, that it was a few mocked and angry men who were already confused by the Midwest eager to locate him to pass the tragic bill of their deceptions and larceny.

Until that moment, luck had been with him, but neither he nor anyone could guarantee that, when he least suspected it, he would face one of those forgotten enemies again and that it would be time for him to be held accountable for his conduct.

For the moment, the others were very far away, and if not far, disoriented as to his whereabouts and what he wanted to solve was the immediate danger represented by those two daring cowboys who had clearly demonstrated their willingness not to forgive him for the tragic task that he had done. intended to do them.

Given how the situation presented itself, there was no room for palliations. Either he killed or they killed him, and between the two the choice was not in doubt.

With Stupp dead, he needed a tough, unscrupulous man capable of organizing some trap that at least Caleb and Corny would fall into; As for Tyson, he gave him very little importance and with his protectors gone, getting rid of him was a simple matter.

After much thought and planning, he came to the conclusion that the only man capable of solving that dangerous ballot for him was Warwich Skene, a rock-hard gunman, who was currently charging the cheap for the gambling dens of Tombstone.

Skene was the only man who could stand up to Caleb and Corny, but he was going to pay him well. Something painful for Grant who was stingy with greed, but now, when it came to his life, he couldn't look on selfishly.

And when he got up the next morning, he summoned one of those who had mounted his personal guard at the gambling den the night before and ordered him:

"James, I need you to take a ride to Tombstone and look there for Warwich Skene. It will not be difficult for you to locate him and when you do, tell him for me that I have a job for him that will pay him well. Please beg him to come see me as soon as possible, because the matter is urgent.

The plaintiff wasted no time and riding on horseback, he took a fifteen-mile ride to the mining town in search of the life spar.

She had to wait until it was dark to look for him in the most rude gambling dens in the town and when shortly before midnight she discovered him, she gave him the order.

Skene, who was in a bad time for money, replied:

"You are on time, boy. You say the thing is urgent? Well, by then it's late.

And without wasting a minute, he mounted his horse, ready to reach Fairbank that night. He would enter it very late, but in time to do so before the joint closed its doors.

The animation faded when Skene entered the Tombstone Bar. Only the stragglers remained and before long the lights would be turned off and the establishment closed.

Grant was still locked in his inner rooms with little to see and had to be alerted to the presence of the gunman.

This one was well known at Fairbank. He had been there for a while sowing terror in the vice premises and if he disappeared it was because he understood that in the large mining town there were more horizons for his activities.

When Betty saw him enter and later go inside called by Grant, she seemed to guess the reason for his presence and an unhealthy inspiration prompted her to run to the small locker where he was dressing to try to find out about the interview if it was held in the office .

In his haste he did not even have time to tell Lamore of his decision. The gambler was still cold and indifferent to the roulette wheel, hoping that the few recalcitrant players in the game would decide to end the game.

Grant was waiting nervously for the gunman. The latter, with a boastful and aggressive air, entered the office, saying:

"Hi, Phelps, what has your gut broken to send for me, in such a rush? I find him like a scared rabbit.

Grant gritted his teeth, replying:

"Scared, no. I'm not afraid of anyone when it comes to equal forces, but I'm not such a fool to expose myself when my enemies outnumber me.

"Already. A job for my pretty revolver, isn't it?

"That's right, Skene.

"Well, tell me what it is and how much you are going to pay.

"Two types of care, in particular, hinder me. If there are three, better, but with two I am satisfied.

"And for two enemies you feel so cowed?

"They are on guard, they stalk me fiercely and if I moved to try to confront them in person, they would not let me take the initiative.

"Well, there you with your things. The fact is that I have to send you to hell and you are going to pay the travel expenses. Tell me, who is it and what will you pay?

"You must know them. Their names are Corny Wiggins and Caleb Sintair. The other one who can enter the raid is a smug young man named Tyson, whom those two toads protect.

"Very good, Grant; Start by acknowledging that those two guys aren't exactly two unhappy swallows. They know where the revolver hits them and they also know how to use it.

"I have not denied it, Skene.

"I'm glad, because everything has its price according to its value. Those two men are careful and their death is worth more than that of others. How much is the rate?

"I want to be generous and I'll give you two hundred dollars

"The amount is acceptable, but double it and if that other guy comes into the matter, we can add a hundred dollars for him. Total, five hundred if I book all three.

"It's a lot, Skene. I'm bad at funds and ...

"To hell with you and your selfishness. If I were to gun down with you now and open that box on your back, I'd take out a few thousand of it. That amount, or you will kill your own fleas.

Grant, sweating like a condemned man under the pressure of the gunman, ended up accepting with a deep sigh.

"Okay," he said, "the five hundred, but when you've done the job.

"That will be simple, since they will not suspect that I am involved in the ruckus. Where do you think I can find them?

"They are staying at the inn of« The Silver Dollar », you know it.

"Magnificent. They also know me there for having stopped and there will be no difficulties. As I need accommodation, I will present myself there now and discreetly inform myself about this beautiful trio. As soon as you acquire the necessary details so as not to err, well ... surely tomorrow morning at breakfast you will find some very tasty pills that you will not be able to digest because they are strong. Prepare the money because at midmorning I will come to collect. I have an appointment in Tombstone at noon and I want to be there at that time. I'm going to the inn.

At that moment a noise of broken glass or crockery was produced on the other side of the partition. The two, startled, looked at each other for a moment, and Skene, frowning, bellowed:

"Hey? Who the hell is out there?

Grant reacted in a savage way. This was Betty's dressing room and only she could have been the one to drop the gadget denouncing her presence.

And a world of suspicion poured into Grant's imagination. He was sure that the young woman had caught that tragic conversation and this led him. to suspect that she had also been the one who captured the previous one with Stupp, giving the blow to those interested to put them on their guard and a savage anger contracted her face. Pushing Skene away fiercely, he bellowed:

"Wait for me here; I will fix this.

And he ran in the direction of the joint.

Betty, as Phelps supposed, had caught syllable by syllable all the cowardly conversation of these two men and a terrible anguish dominated her. Again a hideous crime was woven behind that thin wooden partition and this time so tight and with such haste of time, that she was terrified to ponder that there would be no human way to interfere with the movements of the gunman.

And the panic and giddiness was such that, driven by fear and anger, she tried to run to get out before Skene and fly to the inn in search of the cowboys and Tyson to warn them about the danger that threatened them. .

And in his anguish as he turned and ran, he tripped over the small table where he always had a jug of water and a glass and both gadgets were thrown violently, crashing to the floor and producing an infernal noise of broken glass.

And like an echo he caught the exclamation of surprise from Grant and his friend. This finally disconcerted her, as she realized that she had stupidly reported herself and that Phelps would have guessed the truth and this time he would not settle for just mistreating her.

Pale as a dead woman, clutching her chest with her hands to contain the pounding of her heart, she reached the living room. This was deserted and Lamore was preparing to finalize his preparations to leave.

The young woman, rushing past him, pleaded hoarsely:

"Lord Lamore, save me! Don't let him come out after me or he'll shoot me to pieces. Please...

And before the astonished gambler had time to ask any questions, the girl, maddened, had disappeared from the gambling den.

Lamore was tempted to run after her, but the plea she had made was too dramatic to ignore. He guessed that something new and terrible had discovered and that Grant had discovered that she was spying on him.

And phlegmatically he prepared to face what happened.

At that moment, Grant appeared in the room, decomposed and green with anger. In a rush he made his way to the locker room site and entered them with the cocked revolver.

But a howl of anger erupted in her throat when she realized she was late. Betty had also realized that she had been discovered and faster than he had taken flight.

But it must not be far away. Everything had developed in a few minutes and no matter how fast it was, it would not be too far from the joint.

Retracing his steps, he roared:

"Where is Betty?

"He's already gone," Lamore replied coldly.

Phelps tried to push him out of the way, but the gambler, stopping him by one arm, exclaimed:

"What the hell is wrong with him, Grant?

"Go to hell and let me out. I will kill her, I have to kill her as a traitor and a snitch. She was the one who reported me and now ... Let me ...

He made the intention of pointing the revolver at him. Lamore, serene and dominating, slapped him hard, forcing him to drop the weapon and exclaimed:

"Still; I cannot allow that ...

At that moment, Skene, as angry as Grant, appeared in the joint, crying:

"What was that, Grant?

The latter, desperate and trusting in the skill and aggressiveness of his accomplice, bellowed:

"Runs! Find Betty and shoot her down. She is the traitor and ...

Skene, hearing him, tried to win the start, but Lamore, in a colorless voice, ordered:

"Quiet, Skene; better not try.

The order was like a challenge and the gunman, swiftly, brought his hand to his side pulling the revolver, but he would never have a chance to know how a small pistol had appeared in his opponent's hand that thundered softly for only once.

The gunman, in a desperate gesture, moved both arms to bring them to his chest in a movement of infinite anguish and it seemed that he was going to continue advancing, but suddenly he collapsed on his face, crushing her against the floor.

The small but accurate bullet had flown straight into his rotten heart and the gunman had barely had time to realize where death had struck him.

Grant, wide-eyed, backed away, staring in terror at the gambler, while he coldly holstered the weapon under his armpit, saying:

"Grant, you are more than just a common rogue. Here the rogues are legion and you have to accept living with them, but you are something worse. He is one of several reptiles that swarm west of Tombstone and in his greed and unscrupulousness he does not even hesitate to murder unhappy women after they have been exploiting and villainizing them.

"What do you know about that? She is a snitch, a traitor, she used to listen behind the wall to find out about my business and denounce them. Here the snitches are over ...

"And cowards who brag about being brave and then hire hit men, too. Following that theory, you should have been eliminated long ago, Grant, and if you live, it's a miracle. Why had you brought this snake here, to plot some new cowardice? You are so despicable that you lack the courage to face your enemies. Why don't you run away like coyotes?

"I don't have to give you an account of my actions. Why do you presume so much that you are a despicable gambler who has not even served to emancipate yourself from working as a slave in these places?

"I will answer you in your own words, Grant. Nobody gets involved in my affairs, but I will add one thing. That girl comes under my protection from now on and if something happens to her, I will look for you in the bowels of the earth and she will not have enough head to fit the lead that I will have to put into her. You are aware.

"And you are aware that you have nothing to do here now. From this moment he is fired from the gambling den.

"I had fired myself before you tried. As stained as I may feel, I still have plenty of dignity to disgust working for you.

He nudged Grant's revolver with his foot, then bent briskly to pick him up. Once in his pocket, he prepared to leave the premises amid the surprise of the only employees who witnessed the bloody scene.

"I'm going, Phelps," Lamore indicated, "but don't forget the warning I have given you. That woman must be sacred to you if you are interested in continuing to live. I do not know where in his despair he has taken refuge, but since I cannot find her, I swear to him that I will return and set fire to the den by burning him alive inside it.

Dominated by a cold anger that made him much more dangerous, he went out onto the road and, arming himself again with the pistol, waited, but Grant, scared, did not feel the reaction to go after him and when he was convinced that he would not do it he started walking slowly wondering what had become of the terrified girl.

Instinct told her that the conversation she had discovered again must affect Tyson and the two cowboys, and by logic, she told herself that perhaps in her panic she would have gone to the inn in search of them to give them an account of what had been plotted and put yourself under their protection.

And as the paternal sympathy he felt for the girl urged him not to abandon her but to protect her personally, he did not hesitate for a moment to go to the inn in search of the cowboys. He had to find out if Betty had taken refuge there and in time, speak clearly with the three men.

When he reached the inn, the hall was almost dark. Absolute silence reigned in him and the clerk on duty half dozed behind the counter.

Lamore shook him saying:

"Wake up. Did a young woman come here recently asking about Wiggins and Sintair?

"No, Mr. Lamore," replied the clerk who had recognized the gambler.

"Not even for young Tyson?

"No woman has come.

"Didn't you enter without realizing it?

"Not. Although half asleep, I was not so as not to notice any visit,

"Are those three men here?

"Two nothing more. Caleb Sintair left this morning and must have gone to Tombstone.

"It's okay. When they get up tomorrow morning tell them that I have been here and that I need to speak with them about something urgent. Please go find me at my accommodation. You already know where I live.

"Yes, Mr. Lamore; at Sam's widow's house.

"Perfectly; I wait for you there.

The gambler, tense, left the inn and walked around the village a few times, wondering where Betty had gone to take refuge at such hours.

And suddenly he guessed. If she had not gone directly to the inn, perhaps in her disorientation she would have gone to her accommodation, to give an account of what she had discovered and seek in him the protection that she so badly needed.

Betty had run, in her desperation, down the road with the anguish of feeling the detonations explode at any moment. Instinct told her that Grant had guessed the full truth of her involvement in his affairs and that it would only take him as long as it took him to leave his office and run after her to find her.

The young woman, like a gazelle whose feet were spread by fear, ran down the road raising clouds of fine dust and eagerly reached the first cross alley, filtering through it. Having saved the straight from the gambling den to there, his hope now focused on disorienting him, circling the streets and alleys to get rid of the chase and do something practical that at least deserved as compensation for the danger he was running.

And when after a quarter of an hour of walking disoriented, she thought she had removed the danger for the moment, her imagination began to work at full speed.

He had nowhere to take refuge or where to go. Anywhere would be equally dire for her, and only three men could put a missile barrier between her and Grant's. These three men were the rough cowboys and Tyson.

The figure of the latter grew perhaps too large in his thought. He was a determined and brave boy who had once come to their defense and perhaps now would do so with more enthusiasm when he learned that he had risked being shot to death, only to discover a new plot against them.

And encouraged by this idea, she straightened her course toward the inn. Although the hour was very untimely, the matter well deserved to wake up the tough trio.

But when he approached her, she stopped tense. Wouldn't he be doing something stupid to go there? The plan was to assassinate the three at the inn, and when it was discovered, the logical thing was for the gunman Skene to hasten to go to the inn in the hope of finding it there, or preventing it from arriving in time to put the threatened ones on guard.

Common sense advised him not to expose more than he had exposed, but the lives of these men were in serious danger and he had to do something to avoid it.

And then Lamore's name came to her lips. Only the gambler was his true friend and a kind man. As before, he could intervene with more authority and energy and he had to trust him with the secret of what had been discovered.

He, too, could do something to help her. If he couldn't find protection in Cosimo, or in his jeans, who would risk being shot down for defending it?

Straightening his course, he headed for Lamore's lodge. He must have been surprised by what happened and, furthermore, having finished his work at the gambling den, he would be about to arrive home.

Fearful at every step of running into the bloodthirsty Skene, she arrived at the cottage and called her.

The widow got up to open it and when she saw Betty, she asked:

"What do you want at this hour, girl?

"Has Mr. Lamore come? He asked eagerly.

"Not yet.

"So, out of mercy, let me in, protect me while he comes. They chase me, they want to kill me.

And he pushed the widow trying to push her aside and close the door.

"What do you say, girl? Asked the widow.

"If you don't know, but he does. Please can you come find me before he arrives. Hide me in a corner and don't open it to anyone until he comes. For mercy, I beg you!

"Okay, lass, don't blame yourself. You will stay in my room and I will not open to anyone until Mr. Lamore arrives. Come on, come and calm down.

And he led her to his modest room where he offered her a little water, for her throat was like parched esparto grass.

The widow tried to find out something about what was happening to her. A very feminine curiosity, but Betty, locked in a wild silence, repeated:

"Only he should know for now. Forgive me, but I can't speak, I can't.

The wait was deadly for her, until after a long time Lamore arrived.

The widow came out to meet him and he, with a trembling voice, asked:

"Nobody has shown up?

"Yes, Betty, the one from the joint. She's here a while ago and she came in terribly scared. He says they want to kill her.

"Good thing you came here. Where is?

"In my room, waiting for you.

"Make her come to mine.

Betty went out into the hall and running towards Cosimo she hugged him convulsed, pleading:

"For God's sake, protect me from those monsters!

Calm down, girl; You have nothing to fear anymore

"What does it say?

"That you have nothing to fear anymore. Skene is dead and Grant won't dare lift a finger.

"Oh my goodness! Did you kill him?

"Yes, because it was not a matter of allowing him to kill you or me. I thought you would have gone to the inn and I looked for you there.

"Oh, I had that intention! I had to warn those poor men of the immediate danger they were running, but I was afraid that they had gone ahead and were there waiting for me. That's why I gave up and thought of you ... like last time.

"Which means that like the other time something disgusting and cowardly had been planned.

"Yes, the murder of the three by Skene. This one he was going to try in the morning when they got up for breakfast and met in the dining room.

"Tell me, Betty, how did Grant discover you?

"It was a fortuitous accident caused by my nerves. When I found out about the plan, I wanted to run to get to the inn before that guy and tripped over the table. The jug and the glass fell and were smashed and the noise denounced me. Grant must have realized that that was how I had learned of the above and was sure that he would seek me out and shoot me down.

"So it was, Betty, and you were saved by a miracle. You had just left when he was already looking for you in the dressing room. When he found out that you had escaped, he wanted to go after you and I got in the way. I had to disarm him, but Skene appeared and ordered him to look for you. Skene wanted to knock me out of his way with the revolver, but he was slow. There he was left with a projectile in his heart.

"My God, what danger have I put him in!

"Don't be sorry. Things were getting too tense and this or something like it had to come sometime. So far the danger has been averted because I have given Grant a very serious warning. I have told him that if something happens to you I will set fire to the gambling den with him inside and he knows me to know that I would.

But that means ...

"The fact that?

"That you will not be able to return to the gambling den.

"At least as an employee in it, no.

"That's horrible. It was his job and I ...

"Do not worry. I was planning to quit so it was all about pushing the cessation a bit earlier. Now tell me everything you heard.

She gave him a detailed account of Grant's interview with Skene. When he finished, Lamore made a comment:

"He should have sent for him from Tombstone, since Skene was performing there with more success and profit and he wanted nothing to know about this town.

"Yes, but he was out of money and five hundred dollars for the murder of the three seemed a reasonable amount to him. Now what will happen to those men?

"I suppose nothing, at least for the moment since with the death of Skene the danger for them has been averted.

"And then?

"Later I cannot predict it, but they are not stupid and they will do something. I predict Grant has his hours counted and I wouldn't bet a dime on his life.

"Do you intend to give an account to those men of what happened?

"I will have no choice. I have summoned you here for tomorrow morning.

"Why?

"Because as I did not know what had happened to you, I needed us to find you together.

"You are very good, Mr. Lamore.

"I am like many. Now, Betty, you have to forget that to take care of the future, what do you think you can do?

"I don't know, Mr. Lamore. Believe it or not, running so much danger here with Grant I think I was safer than anywhere else.

"I don't understand you, girl. There is no security here for a woman like you and anywhere outside of contact with these tough and rough people you will live with security and decency. If the problem is that you need money to move somewhere else, don't worry about it. I have earned more than I need for my meager needs and I don't have to save for anyone behind my back unfortunately. I can offer you what you need and you do not disdain it as a charity that humbles you, but as a favor done from the heart.

"Don't say such things, Mr. Lamore. You are incapable of offending anyone and I know with the intention that you make the offer. Actually, maybe I needed something, although Grant has paid me the adjusted and I have it saved in anticipation that tomorrow I would be in a position to need it. But the problem is not money but something more complicated. Grant is a bad creature, I admit, but my life was tied to him in an absurd way by an imposition of fate. I know that he had taken a fancy to me and was in danger for it, but out of selfishness and calculation he saved me from a more immediate danger and the compensation was forcing me to act in his gambling den for an indefinite period of time. We were both interested in plunging ourselves into such an environment to be more guaranteed against the common danger that threatened us equally.

Lamore looked at her in amazement, not understanding at all.

"Can you explain yourself better? "I ask.

"Yes. The other day I promised to tell him my sorry story at some point. I think this is the right time. I'll start by saying that my name is not Betty's. I was interested in hiding the real one for several reasons that you will understand when I have told you all my life. My father was a man who inherited not very large capital, but it was enough to live comfortably and not worry about the future. He had married a very pretty and very good woman and I am not saying this because she was my mother, and from that marriage they had only had one daughter; me. My father was very fond of hunting. He handled the rifle very well and his passion was hunting big game.

"In the Rocky Mountains it had taken on pieces of great importance. Big bears, fierce cougars, ferocious wolves, everything that constituted danger and produced the emotion of being hunted.

"One day, an excursion was organized that included several hunters as passionate as him and they went into the most dangerous of the mountains in search of worthy pieces of their rifles.

"I was then twelve years old and my mother thirty-four. She was in the prime of her life and more beautiful than ever.

"And it happened that, in a way that could not be made clear in a categorical way, my father was climbing a few cliffs behind a piece, he must have slipped on the ascent, and fell down a terrible slope, falling to the bottom of a chasm. Someone who was part of the expedition saw him fall and pointed out the exact place, but there was no possibility of descending in search of his body and there remained, forever, serving as justification for his death the testimony of those who accompanied him and, above all , of the friend who had seen him fall without being able to try anything to avoid it.

"When they told us the news of my father's tragic death, my mother thought she was going crazy. It was a terrible blow for her from which she would take time to recover.

»I was then studying at a school in Sacramento, where, among other things, I was learning to play the piano and sing. I liked both and they said I had a very pretty voice.

»My mother kept me in school for some time without deciding to take me out of it. She was very lonely, she needed my company, but she wanted me to complete my education and get out of there fully educated. My father had left a regular fortune that sheltered us from worries and since my mother was a very good administrator, there was no reason to worry about the future in the economic sense.

«My mother had no family and as for my father, I know that he had a quite restless brother with a crazy head who, after a few crazy things that led him to lose his private heritage, had crossed the Canadian border and was walking through Alaska looking for gold deposits like so many other adventurers who had gone there to try to make or rebuild their fortune.

"My father's friends and hunting companions were very interested in us during the first months, but little by little our tragedy was forgotten and the visits were spaced until they died languidly.

«Only one of them behaved differently towards the others. He was the most assiduous, the one who showed the most affection for my poor father, and the one who did not change his behavior. He remained faithful to the friendship and was the only one who seemed not to forget the drama and us.

«She used to visit Mom assiduously, sometimes she came to school with her to visit me, assuring that I was the living portrait of Mom and that she would be as beautiful as she and never deserted from our side.

But what seemed like a disinterested friendship held something deeper. That man was in love with my mother and with determination and unlimited patience he was preparing the ground to get her to be interested in him one day.

"For a long time he made no allusion to his passion for Mom. A clever and subtle man, he knew that it would be counterproductive to rush when the wound was bleeding in his heart and, on the contrary, he gave himself to the task of helping it heal so that at the right moment it would not open again, frustrating his hopes.

And he had the patience to know how to wait two years without opening his mouth to hint at the least. On the contrary, he seemed disinterested in that regard and sometimes advised Mom on business matters regarding our capital and solved some small problems for her in that regard.

And when he believed that the mantle of oblivion had fallen over his soul and that my mother's young life would demand new outbreaks of love in her breast, he decided to declare himself to her with events of lively emotion. And confessing that he was madly in love with her a long time ago and had possessed the heroism of drowning her love during that long period in the hope that she would understand him with the deal and appreciate his deep affection that he could supply without detracting from next to whom doom had so tragically taken him away.

"My mother delicately rejected his proposals. She was infinitely grateful for her friendship, the favors received, and the honor that she did her by loving her for so long in silence and worshiping that love without fainting in it, but she had not entered into her calculations to remarry and she could not give her any hope.

»He seemed to accept the rejection with resignation and that did not mean that he broke his friendship with mother. On the contrary, as if there were nothing; In the past, he continued to visit her without ever mentioning that violent scene.

»I had already left school. I was becoming quite an attractive little woman, and Mom was very happy to have me by her side.

And one day something tragic happened. Mom had invested most of what my father left in stock in a tin mine in Southern California. Our friend had also invested a good amount of money in stocks and at the beginning, the dividends had been good, but suddenly, without knowing the cause, the mine had gone bankrupt and our shares had become worthless papers.

»Mom had a moment of despair. From a good time we had fallen into ruin and we had to think about how we would solve the future based on a job worthy of both.

And again our father's friend arose. Regretting that crash that had hit him hard too, he reiterated his proposal to Mom. Despite the disaster, he kept enough for us to live well and again proposed marriage.

»That won Mom's confidence. I did not feel any love for him, but I did feel a lively sympathy for his tenacity and will and great gratitude for his offer to prevent us from falling and looking more for me than for her, he ended up accepting.

"We knew nothing about the particular affairs of that man. He never told us about them and if he made any allusion it was to say that he trafficked in many things, had a capital distributed in industrial shares and other businesses and sometimes made some trips from which he took a week or two to return and some time later to return to resume them.

»I didn't like that. I would have preferred that Mama not marry because of the good memory she had of my father, but she understood that she had no right to sacrifice her young life, much less to plunge her into hard work when she never had to need it to live well.

"The wedding took place and he took us to a small country house that he owned not far from Sacramento. He told us that he was going to buy a little house in the capital and furnish it with dignity and that all that summer we would live in the country.

'Mom was in no rush to move. On the contrary, she liked the meek and quiet country life and although I longed to live in more crowded and sociable places, I resigned myself to her.

»My stepfather came and went to Sacramento a lot. In addition to requiring it, as he said, the installation in our new house, he had a business in the city that made it necessary not to lose sight of him and sometimes it took him several days to return to spend a few hours with us and leave again.

"One day, six months after we were married and after his absence of more than fifteen days, a federal agent and a sheriff came to our country house looking for him. My mother, frightened, told them that she was in Sacramento attending to their business and asked what the presence of those authorities was due to and why they were looking for him.

And then something terrible was discovered. Nothing of what he had led us to believe was true, the mask of a decent person he covered himself with had been torn off by his own robberies and it was then that we knew what kind of man he was and the farce he had been representing.

»He was being pursued as a fraudster. In combination with another subject who had already been arrested, they had founded a false operation of a tin mine in which they had interested many candid shareholders, managing to place a large amount of shares, pocketing a lot of money.

»To keep up the deception and hunt down new dupes, they paid good dividends with the capital they collected from new shareholders and thus they had formed the ball, managing to live splendidly on money that was not theirs and for which they would sooner or later have to account for.

And it was in that mine where my mother had placed our money at the suggestion of that man. My mother was confident that he showed her how many shares he owned. They were the false actions destined to be sold to all the unwary who allowed themselves to be caught in their nets.

"What's more, this guy was a vicious gambler well known in all the gambling dens of California and Arizona. He was also accused of being a trickster with playing cards and of having swindled several ranchers in combination with some gamblers as little apprehensive as himself.

»Someone who became suspicious about the legality of the mine had taken secret steps to verify the truth of the seam and with deep surprise found that no such mine existed or was registered, nor was anyone in the market aware of the actions of that ugly man deal.

"When they filed a legal complaint against him for fraud, they had searched for him in Sacramento and caught him in a gambling den. He realized what awaited him and had shot his way through, seriously wounding a sheriff and a commissioner accompanying him. He had cleverly managed to sneak away, erasing his trail, but the owner of the country house we inhabited knew of our whereabouts and had come looking for him in case he had taken refuge among us.

And it turned out that not even the little house we inhabited and which he claimed to be his property was ours. All her life she had been a skilful farce that she knew how to keep alive among us, because my mother, withdrawn and not very curious, had never been extremely anxious to know the truth of her husband's life in depth.

And once again we find ourselves not only mired in misery, but also overwhelmed by the embarrassment of knowing that we are linked to the scandalous and degrading story of an unscrupulous raider who had cheated our patrimony, deceived us villainously, and hurt my mother in the deepest part of his being, giving him so viciously a love that had only been a stubborn whim, impossible to satisfy, if not through a legal union.

'That blow was to be fatal to my poor mother. She fell seriously ill when she discovered the deception and no longer raised her head. Six months later she died consumed by a consuming grief for which there was no possible medicine.

And I saw myself alone and isolated in the world without knowing what to do or what decision to make. My only relative was my father's brother, of whom we had not known a single word for many years and could not even appeal to him for help in the least. When I got a little dazed I had to waste no time trying something for a living. The little money I found at home when my mother died was running out and I had to do something quickly.

"By chance I learned that a logger who had transferred his business was moving to Colorado and was looking for a young and cultured woman to take over the education of a girl he had. The couple had acquired an isolated farm far from any town and did not want to separate from the girl to begin their teaching.

"I applied and was admitted. We moved to Colorado and for a year and a half I lived happily isolated in that sweet and balsamic panorama, dedicated to the task of teaching the girl the first letters and the most basic things.

But misfortune haunted me. The girl died of pneumonia and when I least suspected it, I was thrown back into the onslaught of life without a job and without a family. With my savings I moved to Denver, where I looked for work. I sewed in some houses, I got desperate on many occasions due to lack of work and finally I found myself penniless and with day and night as a fortune.

In my despair one day I read an advertisement on a poster nailed to the door of a small theater in the city. They needed artists to sing regularly for a show that was being organized.

And remembering that he sang quite well and played the piano, I desperately introduced myself. They tested me, I liked them and I was hired.

»I went through an amazing fear the day of my presentation and I came out half graceful. Later, I got poised and ended up being one of the most appreciated artists in the cast.

"It was then that I adopted the name Betty," La Rubia, "and with him and my businessman I traveled many places, not only in Colorado, but in New Mexico. It paid badly enough, but I defended myself with my salary and in the midst of my misfortune I felt satisfied.

»Our last performances in New Mexico were disastrous. The expenses were not covered and the businessman, who spent more than he earned, ended up telling me that he could not continue the business and that he would undo the cast and again I was threatened with misery, because he even owed me a few weeks of acting.

»In those days we had been visited by an individual who claimed to be commissioned to hire a few artists for a similar show in Las Vegas. He assured me that it was a serious thing and that I could perform there as long as I wanted, because what was needed there were beautiful girls who could sing well. He told me he was acting on behalf of the owner of the premises. This one was called "Mexico Salon" and its owner Rich Mac Kinney.

»Very chastened by many things, I demanded guarantees and then she showed me a contract signed by the owner of the premises. It was blank and I only needed to put my name, the amount to win and the time because we committed ourselves to each other.

»I demanded ten dollars a day and six months at least extendable if it suited us, in which case my salary would be reviewed and with that guarantee and an advance of fifty dollars, I set out on the trip eight days later accompanied by the agent and six other girls who had been hired as dancers.

»And my astonishment, my rage and my despair had no limits, when the night I was taken to the premises, I realized that it was a luxury gambling den that had nothing in common with the theatrical shows, since in these it was necessary to alternate with the public in addition to working on the tabladillo.

But something more tragic still awaited me. When I was passed to the owner's office to be introduced, I was met with the terrible surprise that the owner was nothing more and nothing less than the man who had so cruelly deceived us by ruining our lives.

"To escape the persecution of justice, he had changed his name to Rich Mac Kinney and therefore could never suspect that it was the same.

»The scene we had can suppose it. As soon as I saw him I felt such indignation that I threw myself on him trying to scratch him. They held me between the two of them and when I fell exhausted from throwing insults at him and calling him whatever could be called, I added:

And right now I will get out of here and report you as a thief and a counterfeiter. You are the vilest man on earth and a prison will feel degraded to welcome you behind bars.

But he, coldly putting the revolver on the table, said to me with a frosty accent:

"» Listen, little one. If you have little love for life, try what you want, but it is possible that before you achieve it you will have ceased to exist. It has been difficult for me to defy many dangers to get here and mislead my pursuers and you will understand that with my life at stake I will not allow you or anyone else to put it in danger again. So find out about this. I'm just Rich Mac Kinney and you, Betty, "the Blonde." As an artist you have a contract to fulfill and you will fulfill it and I as an entrepreneur will fulfill mine. You will be very careful about opening your mouth by discovering me, because as long as it takes you to do it, it will take you to die. I will have by your side a man who will watch your every move night and day and at the slightest hint of treachery he will nail you several projectiles without any contemplation. Fate has brought you here and you will resign yourself to it as I resign myself. I don't know what he has in store for us in the future, but until there is another solution, we will resign ourselves to this. And don't think I'm just trying to scare you. My life is at stake and you already know enough about me to understand that I will stop at nothing. And I do not tell you more. On the upper floor there are rooms for you. You will not have any excuse to run around on your own and betray me, because I will not allow it. On the upper floor there are rooms for you. You will not have any excuse to run around on your own and betray me, because I will not allow it. On the upper floor there are rooms for you. You will not have any excuse to run around on your own and betray me, because I will not allow it.

"I must confess that I felt a horrible fear. There was such resolution in his eyes that I understood that he was not threatening in vain.

And with despair in my soul I was forced to accept that new ordeal and I was secluded like prey in its clutches.

Although a little more distinguished than the others, I had to be one of many in the gambling den. They watched me fiercely and I always had the threat of a man by my side.

And it was there that I met Grant Phelps. He was running the gambling issue and was apparently associated with Rich in the business. Grant was soon infatuated with me. He besieged me as many times as I had the chance to do so and I was forced to keep him at bay to avoid a new conflict.

"One day Grant, taking advantage of Rich's absence, said to me:

"'Listen, girl, I know something about what happens to you and I understand your desperation and the yearning you feel to be able to abandon this pig. I am not very satisfied with him either and I am willing to abandon him, but not without first giving him back some bad job he has done to me. If you want, I'll make a deal for you. I have everything organized to go to southern Arizona, where it would be very difficult to locate me because that is a relatively new and unknown place for these people. There is the possibility of doing business in a short time and I am determined to try it by opening a store. If you accept, I promise to get you out of here and take you with me. I only impose as a condition that you have to work for me for a year. I'll pay you better than Rich and that will serve as a refuge for you against him. When I miss you and can't find you He will get tired of looking for you and who knows if the fear that you will avenge him will force him to disappear from here marching to hell. Then ... maybe you'll convince yourself that I can be the ideal man for you and we'll come to an agreement. That time will tell.

«I was afraid that he would fail and I refused, but he painted everything so easy, he had it so well prepared, that a moment came when I believed that there was no great danger in breaking that chain and I made up my mind.

My idea was to be able to escape from Rich. Later, it would be easier to get rid of Grant and I accepted.

"One day he gave me a long knotted rope that was to be used to slide me from the high window onto the street. There he would wait for me with two horses and we would flee to Santa Fe and there by train we would enter Arizona and erase all the tracks making it impossible for him to locate us.

And indeed. One dark night after the joint was closed, when I opened my window I saw Grant below with the horses. I tied the rope to the duffel and slid down it, riding my horse and running away with him.

"We got to Santa Fe safely and there, by train, we traveled countless miles to get here, where Grant had planned to set up the joint.

"On the way I learned something that made our situation even worse. Grant confessed to me when I expressed the fear that he would follow us that he would not have time to do so. Cynically he told me that he, too, had avenged something he had pending with Rich. That night, before picking me up, when he had met with Rich to give him an account of the collection for that day, he had taken advantage of an oversight by his partner to apply a ferocious blow to the head and knock him out of his mind. Then, he had seized how much money he kept and we had fled with him, but even more, knowing that he was being persecuted by justice, he had sent an anonymous one to the sheriff denouncing who he really was.

«I don't know what happened to that villain and although I don't have bad feelings, I don't feel pity for him, nor does anything that happens to him hurt me.

As for Grant, he has ended up being as bad or worse than Rich, because although he did not go too far in love with me, you know how he has behaved in the end.

«This is my sad story and this is the reason that linked me to that wretch. A reason for security for me to ignore what has happened to Rich and if he has been released from justice again and is looking for me all over the West.

When he finished, he looked at Lamore. This one, tense, leaning against the wall, looked like a statue of ice. The color had fled from his cheeks and there was a terrible glow in his eyes that frightened the girl.

This one got up and advanced towards him asking fearfully:

"Please, Mr. Lamore! What happens to him? Have you gotten sick?

Indeed, Lamore looked ill. A much more pronounced pallor than usual covered his face and, as if his strength had been exhausted, he had been forced to lean against the wall to remain upright.

Betty hadn't noticed him until now. Excited with the tragic memories that her story evoked, she spoke sitting down, with her head lowered and ashamed of what she was saying, and the fact that the gambler had not opened his mouth during the long story had contributed to her not realizing it. of Lamore's attitude.

This one took in answering. With an effort, he pushed himself away from the wall and shook his head as if something weighed on it and wanted to push it away. Then, hoarsely, he replied:

"No, it was nothing; well, nothing that affects my health. If anything, a lot of emotion listening to you, girl, because what you have told me ...

Then suddenly he asked:

"What is your real name? You have not told me.

"My name is Khaterine Keller.

"What about Rich Mac Kinney's real name?

"Potter Perk.

"Well, girl; now I can speak. Waiting.

He went to the chest and rummaged through it. With a trembling hand he presented the medallion with the effigy of the beautiful woman, asking:

"Do you know her, Khaterine?

The girl, amazed, took the medallion and when she fixed her eyes on the image she felt all her blood flow to her face in a searing wave. Almost hesitantly, he cried out:

"OMG! This portrait is of my mother.

"And this one, do you know him? "The gambler kept asking, presenting him with the other portrait.

The girl's emotion rose to a degree when she recognized the hunter as her own father.

"OMG! "sigh". How do you own these portraits?

"Very simple, girl, because I am not Cosimo Lamore either. My name is Klossen Keller and I am ...

"My uncle Klossen!

"Your uncle Klossen, your father's brother John Keller.

"Good heavens and what a strange coincidence! How could I suspect that you ...!

"The same as me, Khaterine, because what that Potter bandit assures of you by claiming that you are the living portrait of your mother, is not true. You are as pretty as she is, but your features did not make me remember hers, perhaps because with what you have suffered you have made them very hard, losing in them that softness that your mother possessed.

"It is possible, but how did you here become ...?

"In a gambler, isn't it? Whims of life, little one, whims and a bit of influence from your own history, because I too have been looking for Potter for a long time for something you know and ignore.

And since the hour of the sacred confidences has arrived, it is only fair that I also make you mine. As hazardous in another way as yours, but with a harder and more unforgiving purpose.

From the little you know about me, you are aware that I went to Canada and then to Alaska. He had been a spoiled boy with no will of his own. The death of my father deprived me of what little restraint I possessed and in a short time I spent my inheritance. When I found myself penniless and sunk in a pit of debt, I decided to shake it off and try something to rebuild my fortune and went to Canada.

»You were just over ten years old and you were in school. Your father was happy in his marriage and I did not want to be a black sheep to him by ruining myself. I left without even saying goodbye to them and was absent for a long time.

»I returned very hard of bones and spirit and with some money and when I arrived, I learned of the tragic death of my brother and how, conforming to Potter's statement, no one had risked looking for his body.

»That seemed very strange to me, and since necessity had turned me into a true abyss climber in my absence, I decided to try my luck and search for the corpse. He didn't know why he wasn't happy with the accident, because your father was a tough man in the mountains and he knew how to move in such dangerous places. And after many attempts and not without running serious dangers I managed to descend to the chasm and discover the corpse half decomposed by the action of time.

»But I was also able to verify something very serious. Your father had not died by accident. In his body he had two pistol bullets that had entered his back, pushing him into the abyss.

»I managed to lift the body with a rope, I went to the authorities and reported the event. Since this one was old and no one knew where you were, it doesn't seem like they bothered much to make inquiries. But I managed to learn the names of some of those who made up the expedition and by talking to them, harassing them with questions, I drew a clear conclusion; no one was present when your father fell into the abyss more than Potter Perk.

This seemed to center suspicions on him. Why? I did not know, but when after a thousand inquiries and unfortunate loss of time I learned something about you, the first thing I knew was that your mother had married Potter and this clarified many things for me.

»He was in love with your mother, perhaps there was no such thing, but the desire to be able to appropriate your father's money; Whatever it was, it was clear to me that he had been the one to remove the obstacle that separated him from getting what he wanted and for that reason he had taken the opportunity to get rid of my brother.

And I had no more than a single thought. Look for you, look for Potter in particular and ask him to account for his scoundrel.

'I wasted many months wandering the West looking for some clue that would lead me to him. It was not as easy as it seems to get it and only due to the scandal that he created in Santa Fe with the matter of the false actions of the tin mine and its attack on the authorities, I found his trail, but it was so long past that, when I wanted to follow him, it slipped out of my hands.

And the tragic thing was that he was convinced that from then on it was going to be more difficult to locate him, since it was natural that, knowing that he was being persecuted, would change his name to better mislead his pursuers.

On the other hand, straining my memory, I barely remembered him. I had an indefinite memory of having once seen him preparing a hunt with your father shortly before I left, but all that was so imprecise that I was not quite sure I would recognize him if I found him, apart from the fact that since then here, a few Years and years change the physiognomy of people quite a bit.

But he had no other purpose than to find him and apply the punishment that the law had not been able to bring down on him. Whether I lived many or a few years, I would dedicate myself to traveling the West in search of it and nothing better than living in its underworld to have a more approximate possibility of reaching it.

And then, remembering the vicissitudes of my eventful life in the Alaskan mining fields, I set about exploiting the game. I have a great ability to handle the cards and the same I use them with honesty that I apply the tricks that made me a victim to earn the gold that I had cost so much to obtain.

And so, tumbling from town to town and state to state, I went down south with the mad hope of one day running into that wretch. A man of his ilk, touted by the sheriffs, can only live and hide in places like these and I have therefore tried not to stray from them.

But the years have passed and I have been losing hope of discovering him and knowing something about you, because I knew about your mother that she had died when you apparently had left for Colorado without a trace.

»This has been my hazardous and poor life and I could never suspect that the unhappy Betty, whom I always professed a paternal affection because I guessed her a victim of fate, was my beloved niece whom I only knew from when she was little more than nine years old. .

»I do not know if providence has intervened by uniting us in chance when we least expected it, but I want to believe that it is so wise, that it has arranged it that way and this makes me hope that one day I will achieve the primary objective of my life, Which is to confront Potter and shoot him down for being miserable.

Now you have given me some reports on him. I will have to make inquiries to find out if in Las Vegas he could be arrested thanks to the complaint of that other reptile that is Grant or if he also managed to escape the clutches of the law.

For a moment they were silent, looking at each other with deep emotion.

The young woman sighed saying:

"And to think that I was so close to you, and had it not been for these tragic incidents I would never have known it was you!

"Some of that I think, girl. Maybe it's all because that night you weren't in a position to tell me your story. If it had been done at that time, the situation would be clear by now.

"Now what are we going to do, Uncle Klossen?

"We will have to study it. I'm not the one to forgive easily, and that fellow Grant has something to pay off as well.

"For God's sake, don't expose yourself anymore! Enough dangers we have run.

"And we can still run them. Grant is too poisonous a reptile to resign himself to poisoning himself only by biting his tail.

In a mechanical way he leaned out the window. Neither of them seemed to have realized that it was a long time since dawn and that the sun was already bathing the houses of the village with golden light.

Then he suddenly turned around asking a specific question:

"What about that boy, Khaterine?

Not knowing what to answer, she avoided the question in a candid way:

"Who are you talking about, man?

"Don't be new, niece. I mean Tyson. You've been very interested in him since you met him.

She blushed as she replied:

"I was also interested in his teammates. I am not ungrateful, and I cannot forget that other than you, you were the only one who took an interest in me and took my side at a time when facing Grant was in grave danger. You know how you were exposed to being shot to death for coming to my defense.

"Yes, and since then he has been watching over you and you ... have continued to be interested in him. Last night you have been in danger of suffering the same fate that threatened him to save his life.

"It was of humanity.

"Let's not beat around the bush, lass. I am interested in knowing what kind of feelings incline you to him ...

"But man ...

"Look, Khaterine, I already lost the pride of my youth when, because I had money, I believed that happiness lay in finding someone who was at our financial level. Life has taught me a lot and I have learned that happiness lies in people's feelings and condition and not in their money. I have had the opportunity to study that boy and I have judged him a great boy, a bit wrong to stick his nose in this environment, but I judge him man enough to acclimate to him if circumstances demand it.

"What does it mean?

"Don't get it wrong. I do not mean that he becomes a rogue like so many others. He does not carry it in the mass of his blood, apart from the fact that he was lucky enough to fall into the hands of two decent men who will know how to put him on the right track. The fact that that couple has given him belligerence already supposes something and is corroborated by the fact that he felt man enough to join them and expose his skin driving the cart with the silver.

"I understand you, man, but... I don't like this. My desire is to leave you and live in milder and more humane climates.

"And he is the same, although we are all children of circumstances. What I want to know is if you think that your interest in him may have a deeper root.

"Man, I don't know if he ...

"I do think I know that he ... Anyway, you don't need to say more. I think that you would not make a bad couple and that taken out of this hell you can be happy because you are very similar. I'll take care of that.

"No, for God's sake, man, don't go tell him that I ...

"I have nothing to say because he will be the one to say it in due course. Just wait and the occasion will come by itself. The man who feels love for a woman does not know how to hide it no matter what happens.

Walking, he had returned to the window. Looking through it he exclaimed:

"And here they are. They have not been careless in responding to the call.

Khaterine got up hurriedly, but the gambler indicated:

"Do not move. Everything we can talk about here will be very interesting for everyone and this is not the best time to talk about your issues.

He left the bedroom and went out to meet the trio. This one, very intrigued and uneasy, went to the call. After the first visit from the gambler to warn them of the danger that threatened them, it was logical to assume that this appointment would be related to something similar. Caleb spoke up saying:

"Good morning, Mr. Lamore. They just gave us their notice last night and we have rushed to come. What new earthquake is in sight?

Come in, please. What is there is very interesting. He ushered them into the bedroom. When Tyson discovered the young woman, he exclaimed in surprise:

"Miss Betty! What happens that you are here? Did that vulture ...?

"Calm down, do a favor," said the gambler, "and settle down as best you can. I have some very interesting things to communicate to you and I like to deal with men who know how to control their nerves.

"Ours are perfectly calm," Corny stated nonchalantly. As for Tyson, he is still under-seasoned and we must forgive him, but he seems to be acclimating well and with time he will have learned to master them; can speak confidently.

"Well, I'll start by giving you some sensational news that none of you will wait. This girl whom you have all known so far by the name of Betty, "the Blonde" is truly called Khaterine Keller and is my niece, daughter of my late brother John.

The three of them looked at each other in astonishment, until Tyson, confused, dared to say:

"How? His niece? And you pretended not to know her ...

"I was completely unaware of her. I hadn't heard a word from her since I last saw her when she was only about nine years old, and had a tragic incident that nearly cost her life not arisen tonight, I wouldn't have known. He took refuge here fleeing death and told me his story. Chance has done the miracle of putting us face to face and clarifying the mystery of our lives. It is a very long story and sometimes almost implausible, but fate has its quirks and we have been its toys. By a miracle everything cleared up and from now on things will fundamentally change.

"Understood," said Caleb. You have removed it from the gambling den and now ...

"No, it wasn't that. It is convenient to take things through their counted steps so that they realize everything. When I left them the message last night, not only did I not know who Betty really was, but I also did not know where she might be hiding from Grant's wrath. I went there because I believed that I had come in search of you looking for protection and when I did not find it I summoned you so that, all right, we would look for it. When I got here I found her sheltering in my bedroom and it was when she told me her story that it cleared up everything.

Tyson, stiff at hearing the gambler, cried out:

"What do you say, that Grant tried again ...? By the horns of the devil I swear that I will crush that viper. I promised and now more than ever ...

"Don't be so vehement, boy," Caleb interrupted. I already told you that...

"To hell with what you told me. I have as much right as anyone to send Grant to hell.

"Yes, but less chance than others. Follow you, Mr. Lamore, and tell us everything.

He gave them a detailed account of what had happened during the eventful night.

When he finished, Caleb, tense, replied:

"We will never have enough sentences to admire the courage of your niece and to thank her for all that she has exposed to avoid these betrayals. As for you, we thank you for your valuable intervention in suppressing that hitman Grant because ... possibly not expecting the attack that way, perhaps Skene would have achieved something of what he set out to do. We thank you for everything and ... if there is something we can reciprocate, we are at your disposal.

"Thank you. Fortunately, everything has passed and now the only thing left to do is make a decision. Neither my niece nor I have anything to do in the joint and my only interest is to get Khaterine out of here and put her under cover from Grant's possible revenge.

"Grant will no longer be able to try anything against her because we are going to liquidate this matter as soon as we get out of here. He was so cowardly that we went looking for him in his den and he hid like a worthless mole to face us. Now, after this new attempt to eliminate us, we are not going to allow him to prepare a new one.

"No my God! "Said the young woman." Don't expose yourself anymore for me.

"It is not for you, and not even for us in the private field, but for general convenience. You know that we have a commission from some miners to form a body of vigilantes to guard the mines and protect the silver shipments to Tucson. If we left him alive, he would be the visible head of new assaults that would cost many lives and we are not willing to expose ourselves and others foolishly. A hazardous items cleanup is about to begin and we'll start with Grant.

"Already! So ... you will organize that body of vigilantes.

"Yes. We need something solid to defend our existence and they will pay us well. We will have a good guaranteed salary and we will not go through any more difficulties. So far there are six of us counting Tyson that he promises to be a good element once he gets a bit cold, but I hope to recruit fourteen or sixteen determined men to form the platoon and then ... more than one will begin to understand that the weather west of Tombstone is not as healthy as they had thought coming here.

The gambler looked intently at Tyson and commented:

"So here young Tyson is determined to stay and be part of the vigilantes. I understood that his desire was to abandon this and settle in more sedating places ...

"And it is," replied the boy "; But can I do it without a penny? I will wait, I will save every last dollar I earn and when I have enough, I will leave here and try to find other means of life. If things went very well and I saved up to buy some land and a cabin, I would become a farmer.

"Sounds good to me, boy. Anyway, at the moment it is not a matter to be discussed. I just wanted to explain the purpose of the call and it is already explained. Now, you have established your line of conduct and I am not going to try to change it on a whim.

"And you? "Asked Tyson fearfully," what are you planning to do?

"Well ... I have to think about it, boy," said the gambler. " I am looking for a certain person from whom I have had some news from my niece and I would like to know something concrete about her to decide the future. It is a sacred mission that I have been delaying many years for lack of clues and now ... I do not know. As long as that is not settled, my projects lack consistency. So far here we are fine and more if Grant disappears as a threat. Anyway, we'll talk.

Caleb, who had understood something of what tormented the gambler, asked:

"Can we be of any use to you regarding that matter?

Who can guess? Maybe yes, if you ever hear of a guy named Rich Mac Kinney. If they happened to hear about him, the greatest benefit they could do to me was to point out where I could exchange a greeting with that guy.

"Understood. If we ever meet such a gentleman, we will take into account his wish and if due to special circumstances you are not at hand then ... I promise we would salute you on his behalf.

"Thank you, but my satisfaction would be to greet you in person.

"It will be taken into account if possible.

They were preparing to leave the house, when. Lamore, leaning out of the window, backed away from her, asking:

"Have you brought an escort by chance?

"Shooting guard? We are used to giving it and not receiving it. Why do you ask?

"Because if I'm not mistaken, there are four guys strategically spread out on both sides of the street. We have one in front of us under the tailor's shadow, another in the upper corner and another in the lower corner, and there is one that seems to be basking in the sun between some barrels at the door of the tavern down here. A perfectly distributed quartet with only one flaw. Being well known as regulars at the "Tombstone Bar" and friends of our best friend Grant.

"Perfectly," said Caleb, getting up lazily. Undoubtedly the friend Phelps has not wanted to waste time guessing what is coming and has organized his batteries to take initiatives. I celebrate it, because today we had a very bad appetite and maybe a little exercise will help us to have breakfast with enthusiasm. Come on, Corny?

"Go. I was thinking you were wasting too much time chatting.

Tyson said nothing, but gritted his teeth and drew the revolver fiercely.

Khaterine, scared, tried to hold them back:

"No, please don't come out! There are many and as soon as they stick their heads ...

The gambler took his staff, saying:

"Here, Caleb, it's a very useful gadget knowing how to use it ...

"I was going to ask him for something similar," said the cowboy. When people are nervous they usually bite like a sparrow. Thanks.

"I am not accompanying you now" added Lamore "because I believe that from this window I can be part of the concert. It will be some nice fun that I didn't take part in a long time ago.

He said no more, but the two cowboys smiled expressively at him, understanding what he had meant.

Pushing the girl away, who was trying to object, they descended to the ground floor and Caleb, taking off his hat, hung it on the end of the cane, took it with his left hand and, pulling the door, poked it over the edge without removing his body.

.

Two shots vibrated almost in unison and the hat received the two hits in the crown, but immediately two new explosions thundered above them and two screams of death were like the echo of the explosions.

From the shadow of the border and the overcrowded barrels they had fired at the hat, deceived by its appearance. They believed that someone had prudently poked their head out to explore the road.

And the other two had cracked out of the gambler's bedroom window looking for the ambush. Lamore proved to be a formidable marksman, for the two undesirables had been hit squarely and rolled through the dust on the road like two wimp.

The bewilderment of the other two guarding the corners was terrible. They had not been able to see anyone appear and, nevertheless, their two companions had fallen as if struck by lightning and without knowing what decision to make, they were half hidden in the corner wondering in fear what they should do in such a tragic moment.

Lamore sharpened his aim and fired at one. The bullet ricocheted around the corner and the gunman hid behind it as the three friends jumped into the road, revolver in hand, looking for their cowardly attackers.

One fired inaccurately and disappeared, being pursued by Caleb, while Corny and Tyson ran after the other who was already fleeing at full speed down the alley.

Caleb, faster, won the corner and discovered his enemy galloping like a frightened rabbit. He stopped, took aim, and pulled the trigger. The aggressor, stopped in the middle of the race by the accurate projectile, turned spectacularly and went to plunge his face into the dust of the alley, where he was crushed without moving.

Caleb stepped back to join his companions who were trying to catch up with the other fugitive without success, and when he gasped, he joined them, the gunman had disappeared, no one knew where.

Caleb, in a terrible fury, ordered:

"Go ahead, guys. To finish this matter.

He didn't need to say more and the trio walked in the direction of the joint.

When they got to it it was closed. Opening time was noon, but this did not discourage the two tough cowboys.

Grant must have been locked inside waiting for the outcome of his new ambush, and they had to finish him off at any cost.

Caleb, who was the heaviest and sturdiest, looked at the door, gauging its strength with a glance, and commanded:

"Attention; I'm going to tear it down.

She broke away, gained momentum, and like a terrible battering ram fell on her with her right shoulder.

The door creaked as it splintered and its two leaves slid open. Caleb was about to enter the gap due to the terrible momentum taken.

Like an exhalation, the three of them entered the local void, running like fallow deer to the bottom. They wanted to surprise the traitor before he realized the audacity of his enemies.

His action was so swift that Grant, who was in the upper rooms of the gambling den, when he wanted to notice the audacious blow of his fearsome enemies and take up the revolver to cut them off, already the three had gained the corridor and reached the narrow staircase leading to the top.

Caleb, skilled in all tricks, had raised a heavy stool as he advanced and, grasping it with his left hand, had positioned it so that it would serve as a shield, putting it in front of him. He was leading the pack, climbing the steps four at a time.

A startled Grant, he left the bedroom and, hearing the sound of the trio's loud footsteps, shot forward toward the stairwell. Caleb's trickery saved him from taking the lead head-on, for the first two projectiles Grant fired cruelly dug into the heavy seat without hitting him.

But the cowboy's response was deadly. With his right hand he quickly emptied the entire contents of his colt.

Phelps, struck in the chest by the spray of lead, leaned forward with an agonized groan and rolled down the steps until he landed between the cowboy's feet where he was stopped. Caleb, just in case, activated the armed arm of the heavy gadget and dropped it with terrible force on the head of his enemy.

But this excess of security was no longer necessary. Grant had been struck dead and they had nothing to fear from him.

The cowboy backed off saying:

"Okay, guys, business over. I think this has been easier than anyone imagined. It sucks to have to fight such minor enemies.

"Sure, because you cheated," Corny laughed. Why didn't you warn him that the stool wasn't exactly your hard head? Of course, if the bullets had struck her, she would not have achieved anything either.

"The same as if they had hit you on the tongue.

A sound of footsteps behind them forced them to turn quickly with the revolver on guard, but the familiar voice of Lamore, warned:

"Be careful, I did not enter the raid.

"Ah! Are you? You're late, Mr. Lamore.

"I figured. You are some guys who don't even leave the crumbs for others. I did not think it was so easy for them to finish the matter.

"The unexpected and what seems the most difficult is what is usually solved sooner and better with boldness and determination. Grant never suspected that we were capable of playing this trick and ... that's why he lost it.

The gambler stared at the corpse and then asked:

"And now that?

"I am thinking of one thing, Mr. Lamore.

Call me Klossen.

"It does not matter. For me you will be Mr. Lamore. What I'm thinking is that we are going to take over this burrow by right of conquest. We have exposed the skin to get rid of this toad and that comes at a price.

"Are you planning to follow in his tracks?

"Nothing of that. In war the loot belongs to the victor and here much more. This belongs to the five of us and we will keep it. Then, we will assign it to the one who pays the best and we will distribute the amount as compensation for damages. If we do not do it, we will appropriate it whoever exhibited nothing and I am not satisfied with that assignment.

"Well, scruples are useless here. What else?

"Well, I thought that, for now, while the assignment is being resolved, you will take charge of it. His person is a guarantee that no one dares to dispute it and while we will pay a visit to Tombstone, where today they are waiting for us to discuss the matter of the mines. We will return as soon as possible and then we will agree in more detail what needs to be done.

"Fine, I'll take over as the custodian of the premises. You are its owners as long as no one dares to challenge the inheritance and I will wait for you. When they return we will take this matter seriously.

"Agree. We are terribly hungry and we cannot waste a minute. Take care to clean this up a bit so the air doesn't get poisoned and take over the joint to keep it running and don't lose credit. Now that there is no danger, you can bring your niece here, who will be better settled and we will talk on our way back.

And leaving the gambler in charge of taking care of it, they returned to the inn to have breakfast quietly.

The game room of the Tucson Salon was packed with the public that night. Tombstone, at night, became a human anthill that seemed too small to house as many people as swarmed in it and any good or bad place was narrow to accommodate as many customers as they came.

At the tables they played hard. The miners, many of them, came dominated by a thirst for money that nothing seemed to satisfy and they foolishly exposed the profits of many hours of hard work. Some even had their veins already mortgaged and their owners only hoped that they would just get entangled in their networks to take over the deposits and leave them turned into defrauded beggars.

At the roulette table, the points were clustered together eager to try their luck. The early risers had managed to comfortably occupy the seats around the green carpet, but the stragglers had to settle for standing tight, sweaty, making their postures in an unlikely way, since they had no room left to insert their arms and place the money in the tables on the table.

The dealer, assisted by two individuals who apparently were content to watch, although his mission was to avoid an assault on the table, wielded the racket with incredible skill. He had a formidable sight to cover all the positions, no matter how large, at the same time and he did not need to put the money aside with the racket to know exactly the amounts of the winning positions.

For this reason, with a very fast and agile movement of the hand, he would sweep towards himself almost once everything that belonged to the house after the winning number had been established, leaving only the correct positions and on another stroke he was distributing quantities when pushing the magic racket until he settled the Profits.

Just to see him perform in his difficult and risky job, it was worth spending a while at the table following the incidents of the game. For the rest, the picture was the multiform of all the gaming rooms; hard faces, bright eyes, hands that trembled when moving their winnings or recounting their losses, laughter and curses, oaths and grunts, the whole range already known that nobody was impressed by vulgar.

Sometimes someone, desperate, would get up from the seat, threatening and knocking over benches. Before he could commit an excess in his reaction, two iron arms had gripped him, two revolver muzzles were leaning on his sides and, like a child without will, he was dragged out onto the road.

Others, it could not be avoided that the reaction was more brutal and rapid, or that an explosive fight would take place. The timba staff intervened with maximum speed and energy and avoided what could be avoided, although sometimes the end was to remove a corpse with the chest turned into a sieve.

But this hardly produced the momentary interruption of the game. Dead and killer were quickly taken out of the room and immediately the cold and colorless voice of the dealer shouting: "Play, gentlemen", vibrated again and the hands were spread eagerly on the table as if nothing had happened.

It was after midnight, when a really striking guy entered the joint. A man who must have been in his early fifties by now; it had a packaging that attracted attention.

He was good-looking, perhaps too tall, not thick, but tight in flesh, and he moved with an ease and elegance that denounced the man who, before plunging into the well of vice, should have had a more prominent position and an education that should have allowed him alternate where you can learn certain manners that no one is able to improvise.

His face was attractive, dark in complexion, with large gray eyes, a perfect nose and a mustache with some very neat silver strands that made his figure more attractive.

He was elegantly dressed in a loose brown jacket, a brown double-breasted waistcoat, gray suede trousers encased in long leggings, and a white soft-collared shirt with a butterfly-shaped scarf. His hat was the color of a jacket, supple and round, and his belt was girded around his hips with a .45 colt of black and polished handles.

He moved with arrogance and the inquisitive look in his eyes was like that of the eagle capable of encompassing everything around him at a single glance.

Leaving the revolving door behind him, he paused for a moment with his hand resting on his hip next to the revolver and his gaze straight ahead, searching the place. Some regulars looked at him curiously for a moment, then ignored him. Nobody knew him, but by his appearance, his impertinent air and his poise, he denounced that he was there like a fish in water.

When he had gone through the room without apparently finding anyone he was interested in, he advanced to the counter, took out a silver dollar, tossed it into the air with his thumb, forcing it to spin in the air, and the coin landed on it. the tin on the counter.

"Whiskey! He asked in a deep, energetic voice.

They served him a large glass of the good one and he sipped it before drinking it. It must have been fine with him, because then he downed it in one gulp without blinking.

Detaching himself from the counter, he crossed the room and entered the game room packed with points. Again he requisitioned the staff and then calmly circled around the tables, learning about the kinds of games that worked and studying the faces of the points and the dealers, as if that detail was of great importance to him.

Finally he stopped at the roulette table and looked around him. There was a triple row of points that formed a barrier and although because of his height he could see the table, he could not find a hole through which to filter to the first row.

Ahead of him, sitting by the mat, stood out a miner who must have had too much to drink. Between the alcohol, the floating smoke and the heat that reigned there, his head had become more than seemed prudent and he was playing in a crazy way, doing various positions and volume.

He laughed, shouted, commented on the plays and even luck seemed to amuse himself with him, since sometimes the racket would sweep everything he had put in the squares and other times it would push lots of money towards him.

The newcomer noticed the giddy miner and after a moment of contemplation tucked his hard elbows between two in the line and pushed them sideways, pushing through. Some turned angry to repel the shove, but the threatening gaze of the intruder and his humanity seemed to inhibit him.

And so he managed to side with the miner willing to take part in the game.

He took out a handful of bills and in turn distributed a few, broadcast by numbers, a plenary session, two paintings, several horses. Something that only with a very good memory could be accurately remembered.

He won a painting and a horse. He put on new clothes again and thus he was playing for a while, without his flow being greatly altered in the hazards of the ivory ball.

Until a sensational play occurred. He had put five dollars on seventeen, while the miner, who was playing wildly, placed three twenty dollar chips on sixteen.

The ball rolled. No one had appreciated his partner's playing by watching only what luck had in store for him, and everyone was eagerly following the ivory ball's jumps as the bowl slowed down.

The colorless voice of the dealer sang:

"Sixteen, incarnate, win.

With an energetic and confident movement, he collected the stakes outside the number, leaving only four small piles left around sixteen. The plenary session, two paintings and a horse.

And when with the racket he pushed the large pile of chips corresponding to the plenary session, the miner stretched out his arm, but the stranger's arm firmly grasped it, warning:

"Wait a minute, friend; nothing to be wrong. You put your money at seventeen and that plenum is mine.

The miner stirred in anger, shouting:

"What do you say, toad from hell? I know what I put and where I put it. Nobody risked a plenary session as much as I did and this money is mine.

He tried to take it again, but this time, the intruder, with a fierce jerk, yanked him from the seat at the rear, making him fall like a bundle on the double row of points and onlookers that formed a barrier behind him.

The battered seeker tried to reach the revolver from the ground, but his opponent, without leaving the table, moved his foot quickly and with the sturdy heel of his boot fiercely crushed the miner's hand.

He separated her bellowing and a new high heel applied over his mouth silenced the curses, turning them into a painful moan of anguish.

There was a stir. The two guards who looked after the table came to intervene and one tried to grab the arm of the person who had caused the incident to get him out of there, but a forceful slap forced him to withdraw his hand to bring it to the waist.

The move was late. The intruder, presenting the black eye of his colt, bellowed:

"Whoever makes the slightest movement I will shoot him. This matter is for discussion between that drunk toad and myself. I have not drunk and I know what I am doing; Now, if there is someone who has to declare something in favor of my opponent, let him speak.

Someone was on the point of saying that this was called in the slang of the game "raising a dead man", because he had seen the miner do his laying, but he guessed what to expect with that statement and bit his lip.

The stranger, triumphant, exclaimed:

"They see him? Nobody comes out in their favor, I hope that what is mine is not discussed with me.

He had collected all the money by putting it in his pockets, while his victim, rolling on the ground, spat blood through his shattered lips.

The tension was dramatic. The stranger, with the revolver in hand, did not lose sight of the two guards and they, tense, seemed to wait for a propitious moment to draw the weapon.

At that moment, the owner of the gambling den, a tough guy like flint, advanced, moving the skirts of his wide frock in rhythm and approaching the person who provoked the incident, without showing any fear of the weapon he was holding, he exclaimed:

"Have you already collected what you say is yours?

"What is mine; don't talk to that tinker.

"I do not know and I limit myself to asking if he has collected it.

"Yes, I have collected it.

"Then I beg you to retire with your winnings. He has enough for tonight.

"What does it mean?

"As the owner of this establishment, I invite you to leave it. I hope you understand why.

"I don't have to understand anything. This is a public establishment and ...

"One moment. I have a dozen compelling reasons to simply beg you to leave. If you want to know them, see them.

And with his head he made a gesture pointing to his back.

The unknown boastful spotted a group of ill-faced guys negligently holding their hands on their hips, and he understood what that meant.

Laughing cynically, he commented:

"When reasons like these are put forward there is no way to refute them. I think I should retire.

"I am glad that you have understood it that way.

The intruder exchanged his tokens for money and the owner pointed to the door adding:

"It will be a pleasure for me to accompany you until departure.

And calmly, with an elegant gesture as if it were an aristocratic reception, she preceded him to the door. When he reached her, he stood to one side to allow her frank passage, saying:

"I suppose you have taken a good look at the name of this establishment. It's called "Tucson Salon." I remind you of it so that when you walk past it you forget that it exists and look for another more suitable place for you.

"They are all so similar that ... I am not responsible for remembering your recommendation," said the stranger coldly. Anyway, I appreciate the indication.

"You are welcome sir. Good advice and a few hundred dollars, on the other hand, are worth a bit of memory work. I knew one who once nearly fell into a deep ditch. He was saved and days later his bad memory made him forget that the ditch was still there.

"And that?

"That he killed himself when he fell into it.

"Well, thank you very much for the enjoyable talk, sir. I liked it so much that I can only tell you one thing: see you tomorrow night.

"See you tomorrow then.

And the intruder, erect and tense, left the joint and was lost in the shadows of the road.

* * *

Caleb, Corny and Tyson had been exchanging impressions with the manager of the "La Esperanza" mine regarding the well-advanced idea of forming a body of vigilantes to protect the stored silver and with it the much-needed shipments to Tucson to place them. safely in the bank box.

The most important operators of the deposits had given their approval. It was cheaper for them to pay a few good salaries than to risk losing the product of so much effort and the two cowboys only waited for the final answer to combine the loose jobs they had done and complete the number of men who had to make up the platoon.

After an interview and dinner, they headed down the main street to a bar called "El Infierno." The name of the establishment was well chosen, although there it suited any of the vice premises in operation.

In it they hoped to meet with an individual to whom Caleb had already spoken on the case. He was an old friend of the owner of the place and came every night to spend time there.

The individual was leaning against the bar, sipping a glass of whiskey. The three friends approached him, ordered a glass of rum and started a conversation, although not related to the issue of the mines, because they considered it very dangerous to launch into the four winds the initiation of an idea that had not yet begun to be a reality .

As soon as they had been served, the same boastful, aggressive fellow who had put on that gritty spectacle at the Tucson Salon not long before entered the establishment. He emphatically advanced to the counter, repeated the maneuver of throwing a dollar into the air, circling so that it fell on the counter, and asked:

"Whiskey; of the best.

And she leaned back against the bar, looking with interest at the crowd.

Caleb and Corny couldn't help being curious to examine the newcomer closely. They had never seen him in Tombstone, although that said nothing, as adventurers entered by the dozen every day, but his type was something special. There were adventurers of adventurers, and this one bore in his bearing and in his gesture the seal of hard and dangerous men.

A new customer entered the premises. He was a vulgar type of the many that swarmed there and nothing made him worthy of standing out.

Going to the bar, he approached two customers who were drinking near the end of the counter and asked:

Hey, Sam, and you, Raff, didn't you happen to see Skene? Yesterday I was meeting with him in the "Vanity" and he did not appear and today no one has seen him anywhere.

It was then that one of the waiters intervened to say:

"He was here first thing last night and they came for him from Fairbank.

From Fairbank?

"Yes, they were bringing him a notice from Phelps Grant, the owner of the 'Tombstone Bar' to come right away. He left around midnight.

"Thanks. I'll wait to see if he comes back today.

And separated from the counter.

Caleb had caught the brief dialogue and smirked. If this guy was waiting for Skene, he could already wait for him sitting down so as not to tire.

But the strange new customer, beckoning to the waiter who had given the indication, exclaimed:

"A friend's question. I've heard of a Phelps Grant from Fairbank, do you know him?

"Yes, he was here a few times and I have been to his joint twice.

Where is Fairbank?

"About twelve miles west of here.

"I knew a guy by that name. A good fellow with whom I had some dealings there in ... well up there and ... if it were him, I would like to greet him on behalf of our old friendship, could you provide me with your personal details?

"Yes of course. He will be about fifty-two years old. He is short, very dark and quite strong.

"Pretty ugly?

"I think enough is not enough.

"Pock-nosed and pig-nosed?

"The same.

"Thanks. Now I am sure that it is my old friend and for nothing in the world would I give up giving him a warm hug. I know he will be very happy to see me and I will be much more glad to see him. You say twelve miles away. Well, by the time it is, I wouldn't be on time. I'll save it for tomorrow.

He tossed him a dollar tip and with that air of forgiveness he possessed, he walked out onto the road.

Caleb, who had not missed a single syllable from the conversation, addressed his companions saying:

Come on, guys, on horseback. We returned to Fairbank.

"Why are you in a hurry? It's after two in the morning. We could wait ...

"We could, but I don't want to; go.

They followed him intrigued. On the road, Caleb realized what he had heard and commented:

"I don't know who it is, but I didn't like that interest in going to Fairbank and saying hi to Grant. Maybe it's someone who had a pending account with him and ... when he couldn't find him there, he could believe that he was being denied it and lose his temper a bit. Now that is ours and if we have to defend it with shots we will defend it.

"Whatever you want, Caleb," Corny said, yawning. It was better for me to go to bed than to gallop, but if the thing is necessary, we will sleep during the day.

They mounted their horses, and in the blue shadows of the night they set out for Fairbank, where they arrived at daybreak.

They went directly to the inn where they would rest for a few hours. In the middle of the day, Caleb wanted to meet with Lamore to give him an account of the reason for his return and to be prepared for what might happen.

After lunch they headed to the joint. This one had opened its doors; There were no signs of yesterday's tragedy, and although the motive for Grant's death and the seizure of the premises was known to all, no one seemed to interfere. Lamore had a pretty tough reputation and the two cowboys helped him maintain it. Khaterine had been transferred to what were the dead man's rooms. She had resisted, but her uncle made her understand that nowhere would she be safer than there, promising that this would be circumstantial, because as soon as Caleb and his friends returned, they would settle the matter and they would decide what her future would be.

When the gambler saw them enter, he asked:

"Everything okay, friends?

"Everything. The matter is going smoothly, but we have come with more haste than we thought, because last night something happened in Tombstone that worries us and we have anticipated what may happen.

The cowboys gave Lamore an account of the shocked conversation in "Hell" and the strange character's interest in seeing Grant.

Caleb commented:

"Either I don't know people, or that guy is looking for Phelps's toad to do with him what we anticipated to do.

"It's possible," said the gambler absentmindedly. In the West there are many of us who are looking for each other like tigers eager to destroy us and Grant was not going to be an exception. He committed many misdeeds and ... hey, wait! That guy, didn't you say his name?

"No, he didn't.

"Could you describe it to me? He asked eagerly.

"That is easy. The individual has something unmistakable in his person that denounces him as a man of care. He is tall, perhaps too tall, quite handsome in the face. His complexion is dark, his eyes are large and gray. He looks about fifty years old and dresses with affected elegance.

"Do you not remember any particular detail in him? The gambler asked vehemently.

"Well ... I don't know ... I don't remember ... Wait, yeah; It seems to me that there is something that is not very important. On the left side of the forehead there is a small red wart.

Lamore, with a special gleam in his eyes, replied:

"Thanks. I think now I can tell you who he is and why he's looking for Grant. This one made a bad move on him in Las Vegas. He hit him one night with the revolver, left him half swooned, and then ran away taking all the money that this guy kept in his box.

"Are you sure?

"Very sure. Furthermore, he took my niece from there, whom he had hired and half kidnapped so that she would not denounce him for certain facts. That man is Rich Mac Kinney, real name Potter Perk and he is the ruffian who has been stealing my sleep for many years.

All three looked at him in amazement and Caleb, furious, cried out:

Damn the hells. And to think that I have had him within reach of my revolver and I have not brought him to him turned into a stiff man.

"Better this way, Caleb, because that is a pleasure that I do not give to anyone. I told them I was looking for him, although I did not explain why. Now I will tell you the whole story so that you understand why.

The gambler told them all the odyssey of his niece and his own. When he finished the story, he added:

"Now you will understand why I want to be the one to avenge in person the death of my poor brother and the outrages that this guy did to my sister-in-law and my niece.

"We can see it," Corny intervened, "but ... have you ever thought that things don't always turn out the way you want them to?" That man has come across as very dangerous.

"And it is, but I'm not afraid of it. All I want is not to kill him before I tell him how much I have to say. Dry death is not enough for him and I need to recreate in his panic and throw all the poison that I keep in my soul at his face.

"Well, we will try to help you. A guy like that doesn't deserve to be treated decently. What is certain is that he will show up tonight and we will all be here to give him a dignified reception.

And this agreed, they left to return just after dark.

* * *

The night started quiet. The place was very busy and nothing seemed to disturb the calm in it reigning.

Khaterine remained hidden in the inner rooms of the gambling den. Lamore, already possessed of an icy calm that made him extremely dangerous, since it seemed that he had shed his nerves despite the tragic moment he was living, walked negligently through the room, while the two cowboys and Tyson, like any three clients, were they leaned against the bar, pretended to drink and were only aware of the revolving door and of all who entered.

Until, around midnight, Rich showed up at the store.

In keeping with her custom, she took a keen glance over the entire venue as she walked in and, failing to spot Grant, walked over to the bar, tossed her coin dancing in the air, and ordered whiskey.

Lamore, with slow and calm steps, advanced towards him and Rich, being served, asked:

"Could you tell me if the owner is there?"

Lamore approached stating:

"I am the owner, what did he want?

"You? Excuse me; I had been assured that this joint was owned by a certain Grant Phelps and you are not like him.

"In fact, I don't look like him at all and at this moment I don't want to look like him either, because the poor man must be uglier than he was. We buried him yesterday.

"What… did they… bury him yesterday?

"Yes. He had the misfortune to stumble upon half a dozen ounces of lead and … died of indigestion.

"Damn the hells! Who did it?

"What difference does it make? The only one who might be interested was Grant and he barely had time to find out.

"That will be your belief, but not mine. Grant was something that belonged to me and I hate that my prey was stolen.

"If we had guessed that he had such an interest in it, we might have kept it for him.

"Were you his partner in the business? Rich asked.

"Not. He was playing here in front of the roulette wheel.

"So ... You claimed to be the owner.

"Indeed. The loot is for the victors and since poor Grant had no direct heirs then

…

"One moment. This must be clarified, because I have an indisputable right, at least to a part of this gambling den.

"Really? I would appreciate it if you could prove it.

"I can tell you one thing. Grant stole fifteen thousand dollars from me in Vegas. He was my partner and he ran the game. One night, when I turned around, he took me confidently and applied a terrible blow to the head, knocking me out of my mind and taking all the money I had. The signal is still here, as you can see.

And he took off his hat showing the scar.

"Very interesting. Didn't he steal more than money?

"Well, he took something else, but that is of a particular nature, why was he asking?

"Because here he arrived with a very pretty girl and ... I supposed that perhaps ... well ... the girl was also part of the loot.

"How? You mean Betty, "the Blonde"?

"Well yeah, I mean her.

"Oh! Where is the girl?

"In there. She has suffered a severe blow with the death of her protector and is heartbroken.

"So heartbroken, huh? Listen, I make you a proposition. I renounce to be compensated for the money Grant stole from me and I will transfer the premises to him if he gives me Betty in exchange.

"For me ... but what if she doesn't want to?

"That is my business. You make him go out and the rest I'll fix it.

"I do not know, as up to now I have not traded with blacks or women, I find that a bit violent. Doesn't it take over? I can call the girl, make her go out and if she is happy to leave here in your company, well ... there will be no objection to her leaving.

"It's the same," Rich roared. I have an indisputable claim on her because I am ... her stepfather.

"Ah! A novelty. His stepfather. Then your name is Potter Perk.

He stiffened when he heard her real name. Ready to pull the revolver, he roared:

Who has given you that name?

"She herself. He told me a very strange story.

"A lie. My name is Rich Mac Kinney, nothing more.

"They call me Cosimo Lamore, but my name is only Klossen Keller. Have you never heard of me?

Potter, hearing the name, understood many things and made a swift gesture to bring his hand to the side, but three revolvers at the same time pressed against him and a hand faster than his squeezed the holster of the revolver saying:

"Watch out, it can burn.

And with an abrupt movement he stripped him of the weapon.

The gambler's face had changed. The indifferent mask that covered her while she held the deliberate dialogue, disappeared to draw a face of infinite hatred, and advancing towards the miserable Potter, she exclaimed:

"Good, Perk. What a pleasant surprise for you to find your victim's brother after so many years! You would never have suspected that the wheel of fortune would turn so much, that after many years and so many miles away from the Rockies, Klossen Keller, John's adventurous brother, whom you claimed to be friends with, would come to ask you to account not only for the murder on the back of poor John, but the death of his widow and the toil and outrages you committed with poor Khaterine. God is fair, Potter, and when we least expect it, He gives us the prize we deserve.

»I know your story step by step. I have followed it like one who follows the path of his salvation through years and toils and I have come to the end of it with the hope that this happy day would dawn for me. It has been many years of swallowing gall and poison so that I do not feel happy about this moment that I would not exchange for all the treasures in the world.

»Since this morning I have been waiting for you. He had news of your stay in Tombstone, of your interest in Grant, and of your promise to come and find him. You can imagine how long the hours have been waiting for you to appear to settle this long-standing and overwhelming matter.

You wanted to get back at Grant. Well, at least you will leave with the satisfaction of knowing that he walks ahead of you towards hell. He was no better than you with Khaterine and he paid for his faults as was fair. Now it's up to you and for my life that there will be no human force capable of saving you.

»Did you want to see your stepdaughter? You will see her, even if it provides her with the last displeasure of her life, but I want her to see you for a moment in life so that later she will be sure of your death. She is not spiteful, but I know she will not cry for you when she finds out that you are being led to the pit. Tyson, would you please come in and tell my niece to come downstairs for a minute. Don't tell him why.

Potter was pale as dead. His muscles like steel were tense before the implacable pressure of the two revolvers that sank into his sides and more than attentive to the words of the gambler, he was studying his two enemies waiting for a propitious moment to try, if not the salvation, defense.

As for the clients, they were speechless with surprise and in a large circle they followed with eager interest all the phases of the tragic scene, guessing the ending.

Tyson, nervous, carried out the gambler's order and shortly after, both appeared in the gambling den.

The young woman, seeing Potter, uttered a cry of anguish and running towards her uncle hugged him, crying out.

"Uncle, uncle, for God's sake; save me from their clutches!

"Don't be scared, little one. Can't you see that the tiger no longer has nails? He came for you, I proposed to renounce what his part in the gambling den believes in exchange for him to hand over your person. There you have him, my golden dream that should be yours has come true. He himself, by the hand of fatality, has come to surrender. If I have something to thank him in the world, it is that he is the one who has come to offer his life to me voluntarily. Take a good look at him one last time, because you won't see him anymore. The sun of the new day will not feel soiled in its light as it illuminates this jackal without entrails.

Suddenly something unforeseen happened. Potter, who had to hide a sharp stiletto in the sleeve of his jacket, maneuvered gently to get it to slide into his hand and when he reached it, with an unforeseen movement he prodded Caleb in the arm with which he was holding the weapon forcing him to emit a howl of pain and drop the revolver. Then, swift as lightning, he jumped in an unlikely way trying to reach the girl with the tip of the deadly weapon.

Tyson, who was staring at him in fascination, realized at the critical moment and jumped in front of the young woman. The weapon found him in the path and dug into his chest almost at shoulder blade.

But at the same time two revolvers thundered. Lamore's and Corny's, and Potter couldn't try any more. Both projectiles had struck his head and the undesirable fell as if struck by lightning, gripping the handle of the bloodstained stiletto fiercely.

Tyson collapsed in the arms of Khaterine, whom he had saved from certain death, and she, unable to resist so much emotion, lost consciousness.

When he collapsed and was about to drop the wounded man, Lamore and Corny's quick intervention prevented him.

* * *

Tyson was deprived of knowledge for two days. When he came to, he found himself in an unknown place. They had transferred him to the late Grant's rooms where, as best they could, they had cared for him.

Corny, skilled in healing wounds, was commissioned to officiate as a surgeon. He diagnosed that the wound was deep, but that it did not seem to have affected any major organs and that due to its healthy nature in a couple of weeks he would be quite restored.

When Khaterine recovered from her swoon and recovered, she showed a keen interest in the young man. She was convinced that with his trait of generosity he had saved his life and this had just inclined her spirit towards him;

And worried about Tyson's life, she became his nurse, keeping an eye on him.

The boy, when he opened his eyes, saw everything cloudy because he had lost a lot of blood, but little by little he seemed to realize everything and appreciated the room that was strange to the one in the inn.

Turning his gaze, he discovered Khaterine sitting by the bed pressing his still feverish wrist, Caleb with a bandaged arm hanging from a handkerchief around his neck, Corny sitting on a bench in front of him with the extinguished pipe between his teeth. and the gambler standing at the foot of the bed watching him with interest.

The boy took a while to react. His confused brain was reluctant to facilitate the memories, until he was able to remember the tragic moment with rewards and when he moved and felt a horrible pang in his chest, he asked in a muffled voice:

"How long do I… have to live? They seem to expect that from one moment to the next ...

Corny got up, saying:

"Indeed, we are waiting for you to die, attacked with stupidity, which is a disease that has no cure. How are you feeling, boy?

"If I'm in hell, quite acceptably.

"There are no angels there who take care of the wounded and here there are, chump.

"Oh sure! I still don't know what to say to myself. Hey, what's wrong with Caleb?

"That they caught him cheating with a marked deck and bit his arm as a reward.

"Don't joke around. Oh, tell me, what happened to him?

"It volatilized, Tyson. Do not remember sad things and worry about recovering soon.

"He was a coward. I thought I didn't jump in time and ...

"Speak no more, Tyson," Khaterine intervened in a voice strangled with emotion. You jumped too long to expose your life to save mine.

What else could I do? Is it that you forget the times you exposed it to save ours? Don't give so much importance to what you don't have.

Corny excitedly exclaimed:

"That's how it is spoken, Tyson, and if you want to believe me, keep telling it everything else that you keep on your chest.

"What does it mean?

"Oh! I was referring to some of the things that you have been blurting out of that toad mouth while you were attacked by the fever. Isn't that true, Mr. Lamore?

Call me Keller.

"It does not matter. Is it true or not?

"Of course it's true.

"But" Tyson stammered scared. What have I been able to say?

"A lot of nonsense and may Khaterine forgive my opinion. You were talking about the girl, you were saying that you were in love with her, that you couldn't live if you left her side. I don't know how many things like that.

"Me? My God, she must be delusional and I beg Miss Keller to forgive me if I offended her. I am a poor adventurer without means or merits to reach her and ...

"Hey, you piece of donkey. If you are not able to tell a woman like this all this while in a normal state and if you are eaten by fever, you deserve to be stabbed again, but with more success. We admit to being an adventurer because you are. Being an adventurer is not a disgrace when adventures are carried out for a noble purpose. As for your lack of means, you will know that you own five thousand dollars.

"Me?

"Yes. They offered us fifteen thousand for the gambling den and Mr. Keller; Mr. Keller is now justified in calling you waiving all part for our benefit. For cause you have five thousand, which is a decent sum. With it you can install your modest farm in a less tumultuous place and, since you were sure that your fiancée would settle for one thing, I think there is nothing to oppose.

"But, if she… she… doesn't love me.

"Did you ask him, you idiot?

"How was I going to ask?

"Well, take the opportunity and if you are so meticulous that we get in the way of asking the question, gentlemen, do you want us to go out for a walk?

The trio rushed out of the bedroom.

Tyson, red with embarrassment rather than fever, I beg:

"Miss Keller, ignore them, they are jokers of the devil and ... they want ...

"Shut up, Tyson. I've heard him say all that. Do you want to clarify if it was all fever, or a true feeling of your soul?

"What if I declared that I love her with all the strength of my blood?

"Well ... I would have to answer him in the same way.

"Is that really how it would be?

"That would be it, Tyson.

"So, Khaterine, I love her as I did not believe that a woman could be loved in the world. Is that enough?

"For starters, it's not bad.

"And would you really be satisfied with this love and with living by my side based on that small fortune that they have given me?

"Sure you do, Tyson. Know that my uncle has some savings and that he puts them at our disposal to start a new life. He says that he is retiring from the active life and that with a deck to entertain his leisure time he has plenty.

"Why a deck?

"Because thanks to her he has lived and has been able to reach the end of his mission. It is not a highly recommended relic, but why not give him the virtue that he thinks he possesses?

Thank you, Khaterine. You are an angel and your uncle a saint.

"Maybe, but don't forget your friends. Without them little or nothing could have been achieved.

"It is true, but they are just a couple of demons with a heart of gold that does not fit in their chest.

And taking the girl's hand, he brought it to his feverish lips, stamping a kiss on the thin skin.

END